A Brisk Walk In Manhattan

Nick James

Chapter One

There I was.. walking along the river banks, hands clenched in my pockets with my neck and chin buried in my scarf to shield me from the harsh cold winds that were rattling their way through the city, I wasn't focusing on where I was going after all I'd done this walk a million times, the music from my iphone drowning out the surrounding sounds, as I pulled my hand out of my pocket to pop out an ear phone to greet Maurice, the chestnut seller, I always wonder how he makes enough to survive, but he always seems happy, today was different.. Maurice wasn't there.

As I proceeded to walk to my local coffee shop I did wonder what had happened to Maurice but then I thought 'hey, everyone needs a day off right' what would I know about days off.. working in Manhattan is a slog, the rent is high, the pay is mediocre and when you're a ..'young' journalist you have to feed off scraps, I say young but at 29 can I call myself that anymore? Either way I haven't earned my stripes yet in the eyes of the more senior journalists so I got all the stuff they didn't want, I've been to more pompous dog shows than I've had hot dinners.

As I opened the door to the coffee shop the familiar smell hit me and a wall of warm air greeted me.. and there she was, radiant as ever, stood smiling ready to take anyone's orders, as I walked up to the counter, before I even opened my mouth she smiled and said 'Don't worry L, Today its on me' I smiled, it was only yesterday it was quiet and we finally struck up a real conversation other than my order, I was telling her im not sure I can make it in this town and she told me to keep at it, she said she'd read some of my articles, I was hoping for more of the same today, sadly it was busy, so I took my order to go, as I glanced down as I took my first sip I noticed something on the cup, instead of my name it just said 'Nancy' along with her number, that first sip was even better than usual today.

20 minutes later I arrived at the office, a tall building filled with young 'go-getters' like me, sucking up to anyone to try get somewhere, that wasn't me though, I wanted to do this for myself, I walked across the lobby and stepped in to the lift pressing the number '37' for my floor.. man do I wish I wasn't a middle of the road nobody around this place, one day I'll be up there on the 50th.. where all the best are, I'll cherry pick my own stories.. as I got to my desk and saw the huge bundle on my desk of all the stories getting rolled out today I started flicking through, looking at the names at the top to see what I got today.. dog show? Hot dog eating contest? A lone man protesting the tree's existence? Then I saw it.. something I'll never forget, as I pulled the page out for a closer look.. Maurice.. under the headline 'Local millionaire found dead in his penthouse'

Even the chestnut vendors were higher up than me I joked to myself, however much I joked I couldn't get rid of this feeling in my stomach.. Maurice.. what had happened? How could I not know he was a local millionaire? I needed to know more.. I needed to dig.. finally.. a reason, I knew it, this was my big break, I didn't care what I'd been given to do today.. I quickly stuffed the page in my jacket, I picked up my work and I set off for the day with a spring in my step knowing tonight.. I'm going to get to the bottom of this and It'll be my name on everyones lips.. I'll be up there..

Chapter Two

It seemed like days since this morning when I first saw the article about Maurice, my mind was still buzzing with excitement, truth be told, I didn't have much on to distract me, Once again I was getting the dregs of cases, cast off's that no one else wanted, I smiled to myself, for the first time in a long time I was excited about my work. I called in at a local café between an interview with a youtube blogger who was 'Hitting it big' and my next job covering a pot hole scandal, usually I'd have been miserable thinking these kids were being made out to be big stars because they could get over to millions of people at the click of a button, bitter I know.

I looked down at my phone, 9:04pm, I'd finally stepped through my door, a moderate sized apartment on the side of town rich people bought their kids as a hang out spot, I didn't mind it though, the area was nice, little to no trouble, reasonable priced rent and honestly, probably the best pizza place outside chicago. I sat down on my sofa, let out a sigh and grabbed my laptop, my mind was racing.. Who exactly was Maurice? I was kicking myself, all those mornings we exchanged pleasantries and had small talk, not once did we talk about anything significant, or did we? I racked my brain trying to think, but no.. Nothing.

Where to start? Sat there looking at my desktop, a family photo from a trip I took with my parents and younger brother Dan, the 4 of us infront of Niagra Falls, probably the last trip we took together, guess since I moved states to come to chase my dreams, I've neglected to go back home.. I guess 7 years later and here I am, still in the same position I was then, What would they think of that? Nothing like Dan.. Travelling the world, sending post cards from some of the most amazing places in the world, he's going to Thailand in the summer living the life, and here I am essentially about to stalk a dead mans life to try and get my big break..

Enough of the wallowing in self pity, I need to focus, first things first.. How did Maurice make his millions? I typed his name into Google, where better to start? That feeling of excitement came back, something I hadn't felt in years, I was actually excited about my job, The first 3 or 4 links were newspaper's with the same news I'd read this morning, I scrolled passed them without a second thought. Then I found something 'Maurice Caspian - Father of Justice' this I had to read.

For hours I sat there pouring over pages and pages of how Maurice started out as a policeman just on the beat, and worked his way up the ranks, hard work and dedication to his work and the roughest parts of New York that frankly even now some people are hesitant to step foot in. I was confused, had I got the right Maurice? It all tied in with the information in the paper? And if this was the case why weren't the local law enforcement coming down on this? None of this explained how Maurice became a millionaire.. Something wasn't right, If I wanted to get something on this case I knew what I needed to do, I had to see Maurice's place, I needed to get into that penthouse but how?

As I sat looking at the screen, my eyes burning from the brightness, I glanced at the clock 5:37am, I needed to come up with something, I want this more than anything in my life. but what do I do? I know deep down theres something missing. How does a sergeant end up a millionaire, then dead and no police officer in town bats an eye lid? What am I missing? There's something about this that bothers me but I decide that's enough for now, I'm supposed to be at work for 9am so I head to bed, unsettled, I'm not sure I like where this is going.. Should I stop looking into this? I think as I slowly drift off, already dreading my 8am alarm.

Chapter Three

'Good Morning New York City! Wrap up warm tod-' I slammed my palm on the old alarm clock I had on my bedside table, It had been 3 days since I sat up all night researching what had happened to Maurice, Its all that I've thought about, selfishly obsessing over a man I barely knew's death because I believed this was the push my career needed. As I climbed out of bed and sat on the edge for a minute trying to come around, I thought about what my next step would be.. I got up and walked into the bathroom and looked at myself in the mirror and I had a moment.. A moment where I looked at myself and saw myself as I was when I first got to New York, A young man with a passion and a hunger for being a reporter and in that moment I knew what I needed to do to be able to focus on Maurice's case with no distractions.

I'd been avoiding the coffee shop since the day Nancy had wrote her number on my cup, I'll be honest, I was nervous as hell around her as it was, I hadn't called her, but this morning I decided I needed a coffee, I walked up to the door took a deep breath and pushed. As I walked up to the counter, to my dismay, Nancy was nowhere to be seen, great I thought, I'm gonna have to deal with the kid who's clearly working here as some sort of social status.. As I got to the counter he was tapping away on his phone and without looking up I got 'Whatcha need man' guess the personal touch was lost on this guy, I was feeling a little different today and kind of wanted to be reminded of cold days at home from when I was young 'Hot chocolate with some orange syrup please' he looked up at me as if to ask if I was being serious, I gave him a casual nod and smiled, He began to make my evidently unusual request so I thought I'd take the opportunity for some small talk.. Infact I just asked one question 'Isn't there usually 2 of you working? Surely you're gonna get pretty busy later in this weather on your own?' he responded with a casual 'Yeah, the girl who normally works here has taken a few days off and honestly if it gets too busy I'll close up, whatever' with that he handed me my drink and I was on my way.

The streets were eerily quiet today, maybe I missed a memo, I'm used to the busy hustle and bustle but today.. Today was different there didn't seem to be as many people around, not that I cared, I had one thought and one thought only in my mind, todays the day I make my play, this is it, if a chance was ever there for the taking, its now and its this. Before I knew it I was outside my building, a deep breath in and I pushed open the door, I walked across the atrium and smiled kindly to Darnell the old security guard, I'd decided to myself I want to take more interest in a people around me.. For obvious reasons, I called the lift and stepped in, as I reached for the buttons I ignored the usual '37' for my floor, not today, today I pressed '45' the editor in chief's floor as the doors closed I gave a little sigh, its now or never.

The doors opened, instead of a floor full of people running around with stacks of papers there was a quiet hum of people in their offices or heading towards the kitchen to grab their morning drinks, I nervously walked along the corridors until I stood outside the person in charge of my department, I took one last deep breath, looked at myself in the gilded name plate on the door 'Quentin Scott - Editor In Chief' I grabbed the gold handle and opened the door, I took one step into the office and marched straight up to the desk, then I realised.. Noone was there, I looked around confused, glancing to my left an incredible looking woman caught my attention, she was tying up some papers on a desk in the corner of the room, she didn't notice me, she had her headphones in, I gave a gentle clear of the throat, she turned around with a shocked look on her face 'Sorry I'm looking for Mr Scott?' she gave a quiet chuckle and responded 'I'm sure you are, take a seat he'll be in any minute' and with that she left the room.

Rather taken a back, I sat in the chair at Quentin's desk, as I glanced around at the walls I noticed a lot of pictures which seemed to be Quentin meeting a whole host of celebrities, I stood up and walked over to one, I couldn't make out who it was from my seat so I got up and as I started to walk over I was stopped in my tracks by thudding footsteps and the door swinging open. I stood, like a dear in the headlights as Mr Scott, a tall, well built man in his fifties with black hair with small flecks of grey starting to filter through he walked straight past me and never took his eyes off me, he sat in his chair facing away from me and told me to sit, I didn't need telling twice, I sat in the chair I was told to wait in, He spun around, looked at me and gave me such a genuine smile and said 'Malone, What can I do for you?' I couldn't believe it.. Not only did he know who I was but was open to hearing my request, was this a sinister trick for me to open up and then be shut down? Only one way to find out.

I looked at him and said 'First of all, I apologise for bursting into your office unannounced, But sir, I have a request' he looked at me and gestured for me to continue 'I've been here now for 7 years, 7 long, hard working years, I've taken on everything, the dregs, noone else wanted and now I need to ask for something in return' he gave me an inquisitive look, clasped his hands together on his desk and responded with a casual 'im listening' so I continued, trying to sound confident in what I was saying 'I want to be the lead reporter on the Maurice Caspian case' he looked at me and said 'Son, tell me why, tell me why I should give you this and what interest you have' my confidence began to grow, he was at least taking me seriously 'I want to show I can be an asset to this company, I want to grow, I want to move, I want a serious role, I want to be the best reporter I can be and I really feel this is something I can excel in and I'll show everyone what I can do' he looked at me, stood up and looked out of the window behind his desk 'I've seen your work Lance, its good, You take the scrapings and at least make them readable, you remind me of me and I like that, I didn't get where I am by not demanding things.. I'll ask you one last time, tell me why I should give you this case' I looked at him with a fierce belief 'You're not giving me this case Mr Scott, I'm taking this case myself' I stood up and began to walk towards the door as I grabbed the handle I heard him stand up 'Damn right you are Malone, and if you screw it up, you're done here' I glanced back and he was smiling tilting his coffee mug towards me and nodded me out.

I couldn't believe what had just happened, my head was spinning, I felt numb, I don't even remember getting back in the lift, but then there I was stood in the street blistering winds chilling my face, but I stood there with a wry smile on my face, a renewed vigour in myself and a belief nothing could put a stop to me now..

Chapter Four

Walking down the street with a renewed confidence, I thought to myself, that's the first time in a long time, if ever, I'd actually taken the initiative, instead of skating by and waiting for things to come to me I went and I took what I wanted and it felt so damn good! Then I thought.. Theres one other thing playing on my mind which I guess I need to stop waiting for, I pulled out my phone *'Hey, It's Lance, From the coffee shop? I was just wondering if you'd like to meet up sometime? I called by today to ask you face to face but you weren't around let me know :) x'* Then I scrolled down to Nancy's number and hit send, I immediately regretted the smiley face.

I looked up and realised I'd walked four or five blocks from the office and I had no idea where I was going or what I was going to do, I thought the best thing to do would be to go sit down by the river front where I first met Maurice, think about everything I'd found and make my next move from there. 15 minutes later I was sat on a bench looking out across the river at Manhattan, I took out my notepad which I'd been scribbling in for the past couple of days and mulled over everything I knew.. The thing that troubled me the most about Maurice's death was the fact he was a former esteemed police officer and there was absolutely no police presence around where I was, this happened mere days ago and I walked this same path every day and it only just occurred to me, not once have I seen a single officer around where Maurice's stand was or at any of the other local shops, why? The more I thought of this the more uneasy I felt, there was definitely something I was missing but what? I poured over my laptop for hours on end looking into Maurice and found barely anything, I need to head to the station, I want to speak to some of the officers down there see if I can get any info, I chuckled to myself, not like the police are big fans of journalists but lets see how far I can get.

Before heading to the station I wanted to give it one last shot at seeing if I could find any connections for Maurice, So I walked to the second closest café, I mean first of all I could do without another interaction with some hipster who clearly thought I was some out of town hick.. So with that I walked past my usual place, which was unsurprisingly closed, guess it did get busy after all, I carried on the extra 5 minute walk to the next café, a quiet place where the staff seemed kind, the place itself was warm with a small open fire in the far corner, I had to say, if there wasn't something keeping me going back to my usual spot I'd be inclined to switch, as I got to the counter I was greeted by a kind older lady who gave me a warm smile and took my order, I kept it simple this time, just a plain old coffee, I took it over towards the fire and got comfortable. I opened up my laptop and I went about my research, before I was just looking for general information on Maurice, this time I decided I wanted to see more about his time as an officer, after hitting a couple of dead ends, I leaned back in my chair, a nice cushioned armchair, warm but reminded of when I was younger and would visit my grandparents, I took a sip of my coffee and was pleasantly surprised, it was good, definitely wasn't out of a packet like im used to in my apartment that's for sure, just at that moment the lady from behind the counter put her hand on my shoulder, startling me, she apologised and then proceeded to point to my screen *'How did you know Maurice then young man?'* Completely taken aback I looked up at her, she was still smiling and I panicked and responded with *'Oh, He was just an acquaintance and I was just seeing what had happened'* She looked at me and told me it was a sad state of affairs, I couldn't believe it, I asked if she could tell me more, to which she declined and told me it wasn't in her nature to discuss others business, I couldn't believe what I was hearing, I asked if she wouldn't mind answering a few questions for me to which she agreed.

My head was spinning, I couldn't believe my luck! However I wanted to be careful, I somewhat felt hesitant to reveal who I was or what I was doing, so I kept it as casual as possible, I told her Maurice had once mentioned in passing he worked as a police officer for a while and I was curious as to what he did, she explained Maurice had been a policeman and was well respected at the time, he was working his way up with his partner 'Shane Hennessey' mentally I recorded this and tried to be careful with how I proceeded, she told me Shane had a bit of a reputation as a rough neck and wasn't always so gentle when applying the arm of the law, she said '*Honestly, they were such a strange pair, he was so rough and Maurice was kind and gentle, even when enforcing the law he was tactful and respectful*' I couldn't help but feel 'Mary' as I read on her name badge, was holding back but at this point I was willing to take what I could get! Before I could get another question out a young couple came in and was looking to be served, I thanked Mary for her time and gave her a smile as she left to serve the couple, I finished my coffee and left the table, I waved at Mary as I left, full well knowing I'd certainly be back.

And just like that, I had a starting point, It wasn't much but I had a name, I had something to go on, I had to head to the precinct, I knew the police wouldn't be too forthcoming with information but how else can I get information? I took a few steps and then very quickly stopped, my foot was about 2 inch from a stray cats tail! I was walking off so fast I almost didn't notice it, it soon sped off and so did I, so many questions going through my mind but I knew I had to be cool and collected when I got there, I didn't want to give them any reason to take a disliking to me, that's the last thing I needed! I was running on nothing anyway a road block from the police at this point could kill the case for me, and my career!

10 minutes later I arrived at the precinct, I walked in and up to the booking in officer, I thought at this point honesty was the best policy, he looked up at me and asked what I needed, I

asked if there was an officer I could speak to about a case I was investigating, Naturally I knew he wanted more information I was hoping to skate by with minimal conversation, I confessed, I was doing a piece, I was very careful to use this words instead of investigation, on Maurice and I was hoping to just ask a few questions surrounding his time in the force, the officer seemed unmoved and just pointed to a room and said he'd send someone in when they were free, he asked if I had anyone in particular in mind, I took my chance and said *'Shane Hennessey, if possible?'* the officer gave me a wry smile and said it took a braver man than him to ask Shane if he'd speak to a pap, but he'd try.

After what felt like hours sat in that room between 2 hookers who were arrested for fighting in the street and a 17 year old kid who looks frightened for his life after being caught with the smallest bit of pot I've ever seen the officer pointed to me and said *'You're up, Good luck kid, Shane was free'* he lead me to one of the interview rooms, took me to the 3rd door in and told me not to keep him waiting, as he walked away I definitely heard him laugh, I was nervous, but not like when I was stood outside Quentin's office.. More like when I was about to ask the kid who beat me up and took my lunch money in school for my money back so I could get some lunch.. As I turned the handle my stomach lurched, the room was dimly lit and there he was, not at all like I expected, a relatively skinny man with slicked back black, greasy hair, a clean pressed uniform littered in badges, and a ring on his finger emblazoned with a golden shamrock.

'Sit down kid, I hear you have some questions for me' ..Kid.. Why does everyone keep calling me that?

Chapter Five

As I looked across the table at Shane I couldn't help but feel some unease, I wasn't intimidated nor did I feel unsafe around him, there was something there I couldn't quite put my finger on, I didn't even know where to start and before I even got a chance to think I got a *'Well? I'm a busy guy you know, start talking or we're done here'* I had to keep cool, I didn't want to get on the wrong side of this guy.. *'I've got some questions about Maurice? Maurice Caspian, I was told you were his partner when he was on the force?'* I looked Shane directly in the eye, he had a strange look on his face like he was trying to work me out *'There's a name that I haven't heard in a while, what do you want to know? And more importantly.. Why?'* I was taken aback, this is not what I expected, I thought for sure there would be some sort of.. I don't even know.. Anger? What was I expecting? I wish I'd have thought about this more.

'I'm writing a piece about his life, we were casual acquaintance's, I found out about him passing and he seemed like such a good guy and he did a lot for people, I guess I just wanted to bring his story to light and I was hoping you could tell me about what he was like when you worked together?'

Shane sat for a moment, looked at me and stood up, he turned his back so he was facing away from me *'You're about to hear something kid, something nobody else around here even knows about, something tells me if I tell you this, it's going to help you find something you're looking for, I know you're not being 100% truthful with me, but at the same time I can see you're not looking to discredit Maurice in any way, and lets be honest, you aint got the balls to double cross me'* I wont lie.. The last bit really got to me, but he was right.

'*So kid.. You gotta remember this was a different time..*' There we we're out on the beat, I was the young kid with a bit of a chip on my shoulder and in my eye's this badge on my chest gave me the right to do whatever the hell I pleased, but yet again I was stuck with this by the book straight laced goody two shoes, I knew the chief was just trying to keep me reigned in but I didn't need it '*So Shane, talk to me, we've got a lot of time together, why did you join the force what do you want out of this?*' I rolled my eyes, I wasn't interested in small talk and I knew I wouldn't be with this guy for long, no one ever wants to be my 'partner' for long, I'm the lone wolf, I'm the renegade, I'm the one just like the guys in the movies '*Whats it to you?*' I didn't give him any hint, I want to be top dog, I want my name in the papers, I want the respect of everyone around me, I want criminals to fear me, I want them to scurry like rats when they hear I'm in town and nobodies stopping me getting where I needed to be. We we're in a pretty run down part of town when a call came through asking the nearest units to respond to something going down just a few blocks away from us, we didn't know what we were about to walk into but we didn't care I was ready for this '*Hennessey and Caspian en route*' He got to his receiver before me, I didn't care, I was hungry and this was what I wanted, we sprinted through a few alley's and down a couple of back streets and then out into the street, '*huh? There's nothing here? Just an old building? Why have we be..*' before I could even finish my sentence Maurice put his hand up signalling me to stop talking, this pissed me off but I knew this guy had a nose like a blood hound so I grudgingly stopped talking.

We edged closer to the building and we could hear some hushed voices inside, we crept around the back, I could feel my blood pumping, my heart was fit to burst out of my chest, this was it, I'd dealt with a few gang bangers and small time dealers on the street so I felt prepared, I didn't know what was waiting behind the door.. '*We need to find a back entrance, somewhere in the shade, wait here and follow me 10 paces back, don't get any closer, if anything happens I want you to run Hennessey you hear?'* Yeah right old man like I was gonna let you take all the glory.. Of course I played the part of the obedient little partner but like hell I was going anywhere, off he went and as he said I followed 10 paces back, a couple of minutes skulking around in the dark and he stopped, he beckoned me forward, we were at a cracked window and we could make out a couple of figures and someone sat down, I couldn't even think what we we're heading into, what was this 'disturbance' that had come through? I looked at Maurice and I could see the concern on his face he gestured towards his radio and switched it off, I followed suite.

We couldn't make out anything other than muffled voices, we needed to get closer, Maurice pushed the window and crept in, I was quietly impressed at his stealth, I followed close behind, we we're behind some shelves and I quickly realised it wasn't two people talking to someone sat down.. It was someone tied to a chair taking a beating, Maurice gestured to me to follow him as he started moving round to get closer, my palms were sweaty, I started to feel sick, I was nervous, this was not what I was expecting.. We got around 15 feet away from where all this was going down when we could finally hear some talk of a missed shipment or missing money? Even to this day I'm unsure as to what I heard, it felt like my head was underwater all their talk sounded muffled, out of nowhere one of them pulled out a gun and put it to the head of the guy in the chair, within a split second Maurice was out in the open gun pointed towards the men, the men seemed unfazed, the one holding the gun merely smiled whilst the other approached Maurice *'You aint nothing to us cop, once we're done here you'll be joining him'* he said as he nodded towards the man in the chair.

The second the words left his mouth, the man with the gun pulled the trigger, my eyes widened my entire body was stricken with fear, I was frozen solid in the shadow just outside of eyeshot, both men charged at Maurice, he didn't move, zero reactions, he simply gripped his gun tighter and calmly said *'One more step and I'll be forced to take action'* neither men listened as Maurice was about to take a shot, I heard the barrel begin to tick over, one of the men launched them selves at him and knocked the gun out of his hand, the other man with the gun stood over Maurice, replenishing the bullets in his chamber and asked if he had any final requests and the proceeded to laugh, I don't know what happened, something else took over my hand reached for my gun without me even realising, I sprinted out of the darkness and fired 3 rounds, the first 2 missed, the last one hit the gun man in the arm, they both turned on me and charged me, before I knew it I was on the floor, fists raining down on me as everything started to go black I heard 2 loud bangs and felt something cold pouring down my face, this was it, my life over in an instant, I waited to drift off.. And then I felt it, a hard tug on my shoulders dragging me across the floor, I opened my eyes, I realised instantly the cold pouring I felt on my face wasn't me.. Maurice had reacted the second the men charged me, he grabbed his gun and with 2 pinpoint shots, ended both the attackers lives.

We sat looking at the bodies for some time before we called it in, I was shaken to my core, was I ready for this? Could I do this? I felt so useless.. The investigators were taking pictures of the scene whilst Maurice and I spoke to the chief about what happened, the initial call was from a woman who saw a man get pulled into a car and speed off in this direction, we had no idea what was about to ensue, once we got back to the station we both gave a brief statement and the chief commended us for taking 2 scumbags off the street, the victim was given a full obituary and as for the assailants, well they were buried and noone ever knew where they'd gone.

'After that, I saw a very different Maurice Caspian, nothing changed about him and his attitude remained exactly the same, he watched a man die infront of his eyes, and saved my life, me and Maurice worked together for another 10 years until he left the force, something that

day changed me, I was no longer the wannabe renegade, it was thanks to Maurice I have all these badges, I always thought I'd turn out to be the bent cop at some point but instead I worked hard and climbed the ranks, I kept the bad boy don't give a damn attitude and that's what people respect, but I know I'll never be the officer Maurice was and when I heard about him passing, it was a tough pill to swallow, I will most certainly be honouring his memory one last time at the memorial service'

I couldn't believe the story I'd just heard, I sat there in stunned silence but then something occurred to me *'Shane, if you don't mind me asking, why aren't the police looking into what happened to Maurice?'* he looked at me and all of a sudden his expression changed *'That's nothing to do with me kid, but I think we've taken up enough of each others time don't you? I'm sure I'll see you again, now if you don't mind'* he gestured towards the door, I took this as a clear indication I'd overstepped the mark and it was time for me to leave *'Thank you Shane, for everything'* and with that I took my leave.

As I walked out of the precinct I shuddered to myself, I don't know how I felt about the premise of seeing Shane again, I felt I'd touched a nerve, it was cold, freezing infact, I must have been in there 2 hours if not 3, the day light was gone and the night air was chilly, I pulled my collar up and decided I'd take a cab home, I hailed one down and climbed in, gave my address and let out a sigh *'Long day kid?'* said the driver *'The longest in quite some time'* we both then sat in silence for the rest of the journey whilst the radio played, it was a short journey but I was thankful for the warmth, I even tipped the guy, I practically sprinted up the stairs thinking of just crashing on my couch and processing everything I'd just heard, I took plenty of notes and wanted to type it all up, I walked through the door took off my jacket, scarf and gloves and put my keys on the side and pulled my phone out of my pocket and glanced down at the screen.

'1 New Message: Nancy'

Chapter Six

As I looked down at my phone, I couldn't believe my eyes, Nancy? Messaging me? I was so embarrassed about my initial text, which in truth I'd actually kind of forgotten I'd even sent! I decided for now.. I'll leave it unread, frankly considering everything I'd just heard from Shane I don't think I'm in the right frame of mind to respond, I put my phone on the side.. Every fibre of me wanted to read that message, but now wasn't the time.

I sat down on my couch took a deep breath and pulled my laptop on to my knees, I had to get this down, I needed to document everything I'd just heard whilst it was still fresh in my mind, which was still buzzing with all the information it had just processed. I began frantically typing away, trying to remember every tiny detail, pouring over the pages and pages of information I had taken down, all the while still thinking to myself none of this makes any sense? Maurice seemed like a genuinely good guy and he sounded like he was well respected? How can someone like that pass away and noone in his former precinct bat an eyelid? Something else was going on here and I don't like it.

Finally.. After what seemed like hours I had finally finished typing everything up, I looked down at the time.. 9:31pm, was it too late to read the message? Would it be too late to respond? This is New York City.. Surely 9:32 now is a reasonable time to message? You know what I have nothing to lose so why not.. I walked over to the dresser where I'd left my phone '2 New Messages: Nancy' Two!? Two messages!? If I wasn't flustered before I certainly was now, the way I see it, Nancy can't see me all flustered right now so it's all good, I took a deep breath and unlocked my phone.

'Nancy 14:58

Hey Lance, Took you a little longer to text than I expected, I was worried I was too forward and I'd put you off! Meeting up sounds good, let me know when you're free :) x'

Ok, message number 1 wasn't as bad as expected, infact.. It put quite the smile on my face, Nancy is the first girl I've even tried to pursue since being in New York.. In my early days I was slightly intimidated by how the girls were but nowadays I'm used to it and honestly, I don't like how the girls are but Nancy is different.. Far more down to earth and she always seemed so sweet and kind, I'm definitely glad I wandered into that little café.. However there was a second message..

'Nancy 21:18

Are you free tonight? x'

I couldn't believe what I was reading, I re-read the message 4 or 5 times.. The words didn't change, I hastily text back, hoping I wasn't too late, hoping I hadn't missed my chance..

'Hey Nancy, Sorry for the late response! Work had me snowed under today, I'm free all night if the offer still stands? x'

I hit the send button and I began pacing my living room, immediately remembering I'd spent all afternoon in a small room with a police officer, I did not smell pleasant, but did I have time to shower? I ran into my bedroom put my phone on my bedside table and started to throw my clothes off, *'bzzt'* I heard my phone vibrate.

'Nancy 21:44

Hey, wasn't sure if I'd hear back from you! The offer still stands, do you want to meet at the café? Lets say 22:30? x'

Without hesitation I responded, knowing this bought me plenty of time, the café was only a 10 minute walk from my apartment, perfect

'No problem, see you at 22:30 :) x'

Again? Really? Another smiley face? I didn't have time to dwell on that little faux pas, I ran into my bathroom and turned on the shower. I glanced at my alarm clock '22:02' 28 minutes.. I have 28 minutes, 18 minutes to get ready! I grabbed my hairdryer and blasted my hair whilst trying to dry myself with my towel. '22:11' I was ready.. Probably the quickest I've ever got ready in my entire life, I was kinda nervous, I didn't know what to wear I just grabbed some smart jeans and a shirt with a warm long coat, I grabbed my phone, keys and wallet and set off to the Café..

As I approached the café I looked down at my phone one last time '22:28' fashionably early I joked to myself, as I got closer I could see Nancy was already there, I immediately felt myself getting nervous and felt a little flustered, but I had to compose myself I wanted to come off as confident, so I calmed myself and walked up to the window where she was *stood 'Hey Nancy'* I gave her a smile, *'Lance! Its nice to see you in a scenario where I'm not making you a coffee'* I gave her a smile, she seemed happy to see me and I was obviously extremely happy to see her, she suggested we go for a drink to a nice bar just around the corner I hadn't been so I was more than happy to go somewhere new, as we set off walking Nancy linked my arm, she was surprisingly comfortable with me and that made me feel good, although to be fair we had known each other for some time at this point, even if the dynamic had changed, even for one night.

We arrived at the bar, it was nice, it had subtle lighting and it seemed to be a gatsby-esque kind of décor, but classier.. I could see why it became so popular so quickly, Nancy took my hand, and I could feel myself going red, she led me over to a table for two, it was nice, intimate, there were candles on the table which worked really well with the subtle minimalist lighting on the walls, as we sat down a waitress came over and we ordered some drinks, all I could think to myself was 'here comes the small talk' something I've never been very good at.

'*Lance, I'm really glad you decided to message me, I thought I'd overstepped the boundaries when I put my number on your cup and I felt pretty foolish*' I apologised and told her that wasn't my intention, she gave me a smile and told me not to worry, I decided I was going to try and be forward in my conversation '*I was surprised you wanted to meet up this evening, naturally, pleasantly I wasn't sure I'd hear back from you*' I looked up and immediately thought I'd said the wrong thing '*I was worried you'd think I was being too hasty asking to meet up tonight if I'm honest, but.. Well.. I've had some bad news recently and I've really wanted to try this place for some time and I just thought whilst I had a few days off work it would be nice to visit and well.. I thought It would be nice to visit it with you*'

Before Nancy could say anymore the waitress appeared with our drinks, Nancy had a fancy cocktail, which she let me try, kind of fruity, very sweet and definitely alcoholic, I kept it simple and just got a beer, I wasn't sure if I fancied trying a cocktail or going straight to hard liquor, I was pleased with my choice, we then spent the next couple of hours talking about how we ended up in New York and how we ended up working where we did, I was surprised to hear that the Café was actually owned by Nancy's cousin who had moved up state, Nancy had moved to the city a few years prior with dreams of becoming an artist and how the busy hustle and bustle life of the big city life was a huge inspiration for her, I couldn't help but admire her passion, she said she had been going through art school and working in the café part time and staying with her cousin, then after Nancy had finished art school they had asked if she wanted to take over and manage the café and she could keep the apartment, Nancy told me how she felt she couldn't say no but it limited her time for her true passion, it was bittersweet but at least she didn't have to give up on it completely.

I was telling Nancy about my work and how I was feeling kind of deflated at how I'd worked really hard and felt like I wasn't getting anywhere and how I'd finally thought I'd got myself a case which could really get me in the spotlight but every avenue I explored seemed to generate more questions than answers, I didn't go into any details as I told her it was all highly confidential, partly to sound abit exciting partly because I felt like I didn't have any details to give, at this point our conversation was cut short by the sound of a bell, the bar staff had called last orders, so we decided to finish up our drinks and leave.

We stepped out into the street, the temperature had certainly dropped, Nancy pulled herself back in to my arm as I pulled up the collar on my coat I reached into my pocket and pulled out my gloves, as a true gentleman I offered them to Nancy, *'So.. Do you want me to hail you a cab or..?'* I asked *'Actually, I was wondering if you wouldn't mind taking a walk with me? I'm not quite ready to go home yet if that's ok?* *'Of course it is, I'd be more than happy to accompany you on a walk m'lady'* once again I internally cringed, I couldn't believe those words had left my mouth, off we went.

Soon we were stood on a corner outside and old shoe store, opposite the river bank, Nancy and I began to walk towards the path by the river, we we're almost at the spot I first met Maurice when Nancy let out a sigh, I asked if everything was ok? *'I don't know if this is too much for our first evening together but.. Well.. When I mentioned earlier I was going through a pretty rough time, well its because I've just lost my uncle, he used to work around here, that's why I've been away from the café'* I took my arm from hers and put it around her shoulder *'I'm sorry, I had no idea, the guy didn't mention anything he just said you were off, I..'* but before I could finish she just said *'I'm glad you messaged me, tonight was just what I needed'*

We walked around the path for another half an hour and then Nancy was ready to go home, I hailed a cab and put her in it and told her to message me when she was home so I knew she was home safe, as I watched the cab pull away I smiled to myself.. I couldn't believe the day or the night I had just had, I hailed a cab myself and went home.

By the time I arrived back at my apartment I threw myself onto my couch and pulled out my phone *'1 New Message: Nancy'*

'01:57 Nancy

Thank you for tonight Lance, I had a really nice time, I'm home now, hopefully we can do it again? x'

I smiled to myself and replied *'Anytime, I also had a great night x'*

With that text I took myself off to bed and as I climbed in I couldn't help but admire how strong Nancy was, I never would've imagined all the things she was going through and what was going on in her life yet she always kept it together and looked so happy.. Her poor uncle, I couldn't help but wonder what he did around that area.. Maybe it was his shoe shop, we did linger there for a while looking out at the river and it did look worn down, maybe that's another conversation for another time.

And with that I drifted off to sleep, feeling a lot happier than I had in some time.

Chapter Seven

The next day I woke up feeling positive about everything, I finally had *something* to go on with Maurice, not much and in all honesty I wasn't sure what I was going to do with it yet, but more importantly I felt I had a real connection with Nancy, that was the first date I'd actually been on whilst I'd been out in New York, was it a date? Yes it was definitely a date, I laid there for a moment just to enjoy the feeling, although, I guess overall It was sweet and sour, I was sad to hear about the passing of her uncle but at the same time I selfishly thought maybe being a shoulder to cry on could only yield positively results for myself.

Eventually I'd dragged myself up, got showered and dressed, I grabbed a bagel from my cupboard, grabbed my bag and notepad and set off to work. As I walked to work for the first time I noticed how beautiful the city could actually be, my mind was clearly on other things, I kept subconsciously taking my phone out of my pocket and checking to see if I had a message, wondering If I should instigate a conversation or whether I should wait it out and 'play it cool'. As I began to pass the river where me and Nancy had parted ways the night before I decided to go down to the bench and review my notes, after all it was a nice day and I wasn't exactly missed at the office, I began reading all the notes and information I'd taken down but I was struggling to make sense of it all and more importantly find a connection, was I missing something? times like these I wish I had a mentor or someone to give some guidance.. *Hold on.. There is someone..* Why had this only just occurred to me? Quentin, he was an incredible reporter back in the day before he became Editor in Chief so why not? It cant hurt to ask.

As I pressed the button for the 45th floor in the elevator I couldn't help but think would Quentin think I was showing a weakness or an incapability to handle bigger stories if I asked for his advice? I would need to think of a sound excuse for what I was about to do, I couldn't give away any of my information for fear of the case being taken away from me and given to someone more experienced. *'Floor 45'* the elevator ladies voice quickly pulled me out of my train of thought, nervously I stepped out, looking around, it seemed quieter today, I couldn't decide whether that was a good or a bad thing, depending on the outcome, I took a few deep breaths and headed over towards Quentin's office.

As I approached I could feel my throat becoming inexplicably dry, I was about to reach Quentin's door when I heard a gentle clear of the throat, I turned round and sat at a desk 5 feet away from me was the woman from before *'Mr Scott isn't in at the minute'* she said, pointing at the seat on my side of her desk, I walked over and sat down and briefly glanced at the name plate on the desk *'Aimee Adams - Assistant to the Quentin Scott'* I stuttered and pointed to a jug of water on her desk *'May I?'* she smiled and nodded, I poured myself a glass and took a drink *'Well?'* she said, *'Oh, I'm sorry I was looking for Mr Scott, I was hoping he'd be around?'* I was slightly distracted by her beauty *'Unfortunately Mr Scott is out of the office all day today, Was it anything important?'* I looked up nervously, and I thought to myself, Honesty is the best policy and you never know maybe she'll pity me *'Ok, I'll be honest, I was hoping for some.. Guidance? I'm not really sure what I was expecting, I don't know why I thought he'd even be available'* Aimee smiled at me and slid me a piece of paper *'Ok Lance, I like you, so I'll help you out this once'* she said with a smile, pointed at the paper and said *'Tonight we'll be here, it starts at 9pm, wear something nice, oh and by the way if you're asking for help it couldn't hurt to have a spare whiskey in hand'* with that she ushered me away, slightly dumbfounded I tucked the paper into my pocket and with that I left.

I glanced down at my phone, once again, no messages, I glanced at the time 1:04pm, I pulled the paper out of my pocket and it was the address of a bar, I thought about what Aimee had said.. 'Dress nice?' I glanced down at my clothes and couldn't help but feel slightly offended, I'd decided it was time I owned a suit anyway so this was the perfect excuse, there was a plethora of suit shops in New York, I'd never owned one and the only thing I knew about suits were you couldn't go wrong with an Italian one. I hailed a cab and headed downtown, I wandered in and out of a few shops not really knowing what I was looking for, I eventually landed outside a shop I briefly heard someone talking about whilst waiting for a Coffee one day 'Luca's' I opened the door and was met by rows and rows of suits I was approached by a young guy in his early to mid twenties, he asked what I was looking for and I explained I wasn't sure, he spent the next hour talking me through all the different types of suits and colours. Eventually after talking through my options and price limitations and what I liked or preferred, I settled on a dark blue fitted suit, I also bought some dark brown shoes which I thought were nice, the young guy even threw in a belt to match the shoes, I was frankly surprised at this but I certainly wasn't going to complain.

As I headed back towards home I looked back down at my phone, this time I was checking the time, I'd given up on hearing from Nancy today, 5:23 suit shopping had taken longer than anticipated, however I gave myself a break and thought I'd done enough over the last few days regarding Maurice that having one day off investigating to gather my thoughts and seek out some guidance wasn't going to cause any issues, I decided I'd grab a pizza on my way home and then get ready for.. Well I didn't know exactly, I'd neglected to ask what this address even led to? What was I walking in to? Too late now I guess, I got my pizza and got a cab home. Once I'd arrived I slumped on the sofa and ate my pizza, did the usual scroll through social media and watched some trash TV until around 7:30pm then I decided I needed to get ready, I'd already decided I wasn't arriving until after 9:30pm so I can enter without being noticed, I jumped in the shower, shaved and laid out all my new clothes.

As I stood there in my brand new suit and shoes with my hair all done and after shave smelling good, I grabbed my watch and headed over to the mirror, vain I know but I used the excuse I wanted to make sure I looked ok and not silly, this was definitely an excuse, I called a cab and gave the address, I still couldn't help but wonder? What was I even heading to?. I handed over the fare and stepped out of the cab glanced down at my watch '9:30' punctual as always I thought to myself, I took a deep breath and headed up a small staircase, I was greeted by a man holding a clipboard *'Name'* I stuttered.. Name? why does he want my name? where am i? *'I.. Err, Lance'* I was met with a cold stare *'Full name..'* *'Sorry, Lance Malone'* I already wanted to turn around and leave and I hadn't even got inside yet *'Hmm.. Ok, Mr Malone, Guest of Ms Adams, Inside'* I nodded in appreciation and headed in, Guest of Ms Adams? I headed through a set of double doors and looked up *'Associates Ball'* I had no idea what was going on, Associates of what? I glanced through the crowd looking for a familiar face, Aimee, Quentin? Hell I'd even take Shane Hennessey right now, I walked through and headed to the bar *'Mines a cosmopolitan'* I looked over and there was Aimee, I got the drinks and headed over *'What is this?'* I asked *'Well a hello to you too Mr Malone, glad you listened to my advice and got something nice to wear'* I stood and looked I assume pretty confused *'It's a ball in honour of all the people who have done great things for the city in the past year, I get the +1 for Quentin, I'm usually his excuse to get out of conversing with people he doesn't want to'* Ok, at least I knew what was going on now *'Oh, I had no idea these things even happened'* Aimee handed me a Whiskey and pointed over to the corner where Quentin was stood she told me to go over and told me she'd be waiting for me when I'd finished.

I walked over to Quentin Whiskey in hand, I'd decided confidence is key, As I got within a couple of feet of him *'Lance! I wasn't expecting to see you until tomorrow morning, what are you doing here?'* I looked at him slightly confused and handed him the Whiskey, He took a sip without dropping his gaze, then he smiled *'Proper Twelve.. How did you know? You've done well'* I wondered what he meant see me tomorrow? However I just smiled and then asked *'Sorry to bother you outside of work Mr Sc..'* he cut me off before I could finish *'Its Quentin outside the office Lance, Why are you here anyway?'* I didn't quite know what to say *'Sorry Quentin, I'm here as Aimee's +1? I must admit I wasn't sure what I was actually attending, But whilst I've got you I was wondering If I could ask you something?'* He took another sip of his Whiskey and said *'Lance, lets leave the work talk until tomorrow eh? Aimee already gave me the heads up and I assumed that's why you'd requested a meeting?'* before I could answer someone came over to Quentin, he looked at me and said *'Lets pick up tomorrow Lance, Enjoy your evening, Thanks for the drink'* with that he raised his glass and nodded and was gone.

Well.. Not what I expected, I looked around and Aimee was gesturing me over, I went over and asked why she didn't warn me about the meeting she responded by telling me she wanted to see my reaction and also get on his good side with the whiskey, I admired her style I must admit, as the night wore on me and Aimee chatted about this and that, nothing personal just general questions about how we both got into the reporting business, Aimee had aspirations of becoming a reporter but then realised how good she was and how frankly lucrative it was just being the PA to the Editor in Chief, She wasn't wrong. Eventually the crowd starting thinning out and Aimee asked if I intended on being a gentleman and walking her out, I of course obliged, we linked arms and walked out into the atrium, at that moment in the light I saw how stunning she was, she was wearing a long red evening gown with white fur scarf.

As it was a nice evening Aimee suggested we walked, I agreed and led the way, we walked for a while and then we ended up outside the office, she told me she had left something upstairs and told me I could come with her or leave she didn't mind, *'Well what kind of gentleman would I be if I were to leave?'* she smiled and took my hand, we got in the lift and she pressed 45, I was trying not to look, using any excuse to avert my eyes, I glanced at my watch 1:48am, *'Floor 45'* she took my hand again and led me to her desk, only we walked past her desk and into Quentins office, she closed the door behind us and walked to the window, *'Look at the views Lance, at night the city looks incredible don't you think?'* I couldn't help but agree, at that moment she grabbed my hand, I immediately felt my palms becoming sweaty as our fingers interlocked, I took a big gulp, I all of a sudden felt very nervous and flustered and she turned to me, looked me in the eyes and leaned in for the kiss, before I knew it our lips were locked together, it was passionate, I hadnt expected this but I couldn't say I wasn't happy at how this was going, before I knew it her hands were opening the buttons on my shirt and I was fumbling for the zip on the back of her dress I was kissing her neck as she pushed off my jacket and shirt her dress and scarf hit the floor, she began kissing down my chest and sat me in Quentins chair, I knew I shouldn't be doing this in Quentins office but I wasn't thinking about anyone else at this moment, before I knew it Aimee was on top of me and we were in the throws of passion.

As we walked out of the office, locking up behind us, there were so many questions running through my mind, what just happened? Where had this come from? She took my hand and we headed back down the lift and out into the street, without saying a word about what just happened, Aimee hailed a cab, kissed me one last time and climbed inside the cab, before the cab took off the window came down and she said *'10:30am, Don't be late Lance'*, I couldn't believe what had just happened, I hailed a cab myself and headed home. I walked through the door and headed straight to my bedroom, my mind was absolutely swirling, I was reliving the last 5 hours, I climbed into bed and grabbed my phone, I wanted to set a double alarm, tomorrow was a big day, Hopefully thanks to Aimee I'm in Quentins good books.

'1 New Message: Nancy'

All of a sudden there was a sudden twang of guilt and just like that, I wasn't getting any sleep tonight.

Chapter Eight

Before I knew it I was being blinded by the sun, I looked over at my clock, 09:03, I felt horrendous, my head was pounding, my mouth was dry and there was the ever present lingering feeling of guilt over the night before, I sat on the side of my bed looking at my phone which still read:

'1 New Message: Nancy'

I sat for a moment and thought about it, I had nothing to feel bad about, what happened last night happened, I cant say I didn't enjoy it because it was incredible, wild, unpredictable, all things that have never been associated with me before, its not like me and Nancy were anything, we went out for a drink one time? That didn't mean anything, I put my phone back down on the side dresser and got in the shower.

45 short minutes later I was out of the shower dry and half dressed, as I sat there pulling on my shirt and picking out a tie for the day, my mind kept wandering back to last night, where did that come from? Not that I minded, but there was certainly some food for thought. I grabbed my keys, pulled on my coat and headed out for the day, I couldn't help but wonder why Aimee was doing so much for me? I mean she booked a meeting with the editor in chief for a guy she'd only met once before very briefly and then proceeded to invite him to a ball? Who was I to look a gift horse in the mouth? Its about time I got a break so you know what, its time to go with it.

As I walked through the door at work I regretted deciding to walk to work, it was a bitterly cold day I'd been fooled by the morning sun, I headed over to the lift and pressed '45' *'Good Morning Lance'* I was shocked, noone ever even usually noticed me walking in let alone enough to greet me, it was the security guard *'Good Morning'* I politely responded, the lift arrived and I got in, puzzled, I don't think we'd ever spoke before today.

I stepped out onto the corridor leading up to Quentin's office, slightly nervous at the thought of seeing Aimee again, I proceeded towards his office, as I approached I could see Aimee, my heartbeat got a little faster and my palms a little sweatier, the closer I got the more nervous I got, nothing to do with my meeting with Quentin. I tried to look and seem as confident as possible I walked up to Aimee's desk.

'Hi Aimee, I was wondering if Quentin was ready for me yet?' she looked up at me and smiled *'Morning Lance, yes feel free to go in, oh and by the way take these'* she handed me 2 take out coffee's, I smiled at her and thanked her before turning towards Quentin's office, I glanced down at the coffee's one had a 'Q' and the other an 'L' then the familiar twang of guilt came back, these were from Nancy's place, I couldn't think about that now, I needed Quentin's help so I knocked on the door *'Come in'* I opened the door and saw Quentin, truth be told he'd definitely looked better, I also couldn't help but glance at his chair and recall last nights after hours work. I took a seat opposite him and handed him the coffee Aimee got me *'Lance, you're going to do well here if you keep this up'* he said as he took the coffee from my hand he took a sip, put the cup down on his desk sat back and looked at me with an intense look *'What is it I can do for you then Lance?'* He clasped his hands together and looked expectantly at me, I didn't really know what to say or to ask the words kind of fell out *'Mr Scott, I'm hitting wall after wall with my research and I'm not sure exactly how to proceed, I feel like every time I start to get somewhere I end up at a brick wall where my investigation seems to get stopped in its tracks, I know I'm up to the task and I know I can get this story but.. I was wondering if you had any guidance for me?'* Quentin drew in a deep breath and stood up,

he turned around and began looking out of his window, he didn't say anything for a minute or two and honestly, that worried me, *'Here's the thing Lance, I trust you to get this done, I have every confidence you'll get the full story, everyone finds their own way, I cant tell you how to get what you want, this is your story you need to push through and get the information you're looking for, these are the stories that will make you into a reporter or you'll find out dog shows are where you belong'* I was in a stunned silence, I don't know what I expected, but it certainly wasn't that, although I guess I knew I couldn't rely on Quentin to babysit me through this, he's testing me *'Mr Scott, you're right, I need to find my way, Thank you'* as I stood up and headed to the door Quentin cleared his throat *'Oh and Lance, if you ever make it to my position, make sure you get a PA like Aimee, Look at this office, spotless, I came in this morning and she'd got a cleaner in to clean my office top to bottom, she's a keeper'* I couldn't help but smile.

Without realising what I was doing I'd marched out of Quentin's office gone down the lift and walked out into the street, reeling from losing what I thought was a safety net, I don't know why but I thought Quentin would protect me, I don't know where I got this from, especially when I marched into his office so confidently and demanded this story, as I was lost in my own thoughts I felt someone grab my arm, I panicked and spun round to see Aimee looking concerned *'What happened in there? You came out and marched off, without a word?'* I realised Aimee had just hooked me up big time not only with the meeting but the coffee and the whiskey the night before and I never even thanked her *'Nothing, I'm sorry, I was a million miles away and wasn't even thinking, Thank you for everything, for the invite last night, the meeting this morning and the coffee'* she looked at me and smiled *'Don't worry, you're taking me out to dinner tonight as a thank you, See you here at 9'* and with that she was gone, back inside.

An hour later I was at the city library, I thought about what Quentin said and he was right, I needed to do this on my own,

I sat combing all old newspapers looking for information about Maurice, I couldn't for the life in me fathom how someone went from being a well respected police officer to being a millionaire chestnut seller? I mean I could understand being bored and using the chestnuts as a past time but how did he get there? What was I missing? I'd been scrolling through articles and there was nothing? A few more hours had passed before I realised I'd just been aimlessly scrolling and then something made me stop, I could hear someone else around, I was at the back of the library and out of the way of anyone else, I looked around but couldn't see anyone, I began to feel very uneasy.

I began to collect my things and turned off the monitor, I'd printed a few articles out to read, I headed over to the printer around 10 feet away from the computer to grab the pages someone grabbed my arm and someone else grabbed the back of my head, my eyes widened, I hadn't felt fear like this since I was a boy in the school playground when the schoolyard bullies were lurking around, I immediately felt my chest getting tight and my breathing getting very heavy *'Whatever you're doing, stop, this doesn't need to be investigated'* and with that I was thrown to the floor, I immediately span my head around, but it was too late, they were gone, what had just happened? This confirms what I already suspected, there is more to this than on the face of things, should I be worried? I mean if they know what I'm doing then they know I've spoken to Shane Hennessey? I decided it was time to revisit Shane, see if I could get anything else from him.

As I sat on the steps of the library thinking to myself what in the hell just happened, I needed to plan out my next moves carefully, I know I need to see Shane again, sooner rather than later, Do I report what just happened to him? Do I keep it to myself for now? I looked down at my watch 18:22, I think the best thing to do for now is head home get myself ready for dinner tonight with Aimee and re-visit this in the morning, I was far too shook up to go see Shane right now.

A couple of hours later and here I was, stood outside work trying not to think about what had happened this evening, I wanted to put it out of my mind for now and see what tonight brought, I was wearing the new shoes and belt I got for the ball yesterday and I was wearing jeans and a smart shirt under my coat, I didn't have a clue where we were going so I went somewhere in the middle, A cab pulled up and outstepped Aimee, I couldn't believe it, she looked amazing, I smiled and hugged her *'Hey Aimee, you look amazing' 'Well aren't you the charmer Lance, you don't look too bad yourself'* I could immediately feel my face going red, she linked my arm and lead the way.

We ended up around a 15 minute walk away from the office, we had general nice chit chat on the way there, we walked up to the door of a fancy looking Italian, I held the door open Aimee smiled and walked in *'Table for 2 under Aimee Adams'* she said as we walked in, *'right this way'* said the host as he lead us to our table, I looked around, this restaurant was definitely not anywhere I'd ever eaten before, I didn't even recognise it, it looked too established to be new, as we got to our table and the waiter took our coats, It very quickly occurred to me I was desperate to visit the restroom, I excused myself from Aimee and headed to the restroom, After I'd finished and washed my hands I stepped out of the door and found myself walking directly into someone, I quickly apologised and looked down.

'Nancy?'

'Good to see you Lance, What brings you here?'

My heart sank once again.

Chapter Nine

Typical, this is just my luck, of all the places to see Nancy again it had to be here and now, luckily for me I was always good at thinking on my feet.

'I'm actually at a meeting with someone from work, who knows, maybe I'll finally be on the big stories' I said with a small laugh, hoping Nancy bought it *'What about you?'* hoping to take the conversation away from me.

'I'm actually here with some family, I can't say I've ever been here before, but I always like to try new things'

'I agr..' before I could finish Nancy continued *'I haven't heard from you since we met that evening, I hope I didn't do anything?'*

I was caught off guard, I didn't expect her to mention my lack of communication *'You haven't? I thought it was me, I haven't heard from you since that night either, I assumed I'd done something?'* I lied, I hoped my face wasn't giving anything away, I never was much of a good liar.

'Oh?' Nancy replied puzzled *'I did send you a message the other day?'* she pulled out her phone and scrolled briefly *'The message says it sent? I'm sorry Lance, here I am keeping you when you've already told me you're at a meeting and I suppose I really should be getting back to my family, call me sometime?'* and with that she was gone, I couldn't believe how that panned out, I hastily got back to the table where Aimee was sat, I took my seat and saw a beer and a fancy cocktail, I leant across and took the cocktail *'How thoughtful!'* I said as I went to take a sip looking at the surprised look on Aimee's face, before the glass reached my lips I smiled and put the cocktail back

down in front of her, she giggled at my poor attempt at humour and I took a drink of the beer to disguise my scanning of the room Nancy's table wasn't anywhere in sight.

The waiter who took our coats came back and asked if we were ready to order, after my traumatising day I decided I'd treat myself, *'Sirloin Steak for me please, Medium Rare' 'And for the lady?'* he asked, Aimee ordered Lobster with all the trimmings, I had no idea what all the trimmings were but I regretted not asking for them too, he took our menu's and left. I looked across the table and Aimee was running her finger around the rim of her cocktail glass *'Everything Ok?'* I asked tentatively *'Oh, Sorry, Yes'* before I could answer she carried on *'So who was the girl you were chatting to on your way back, Hope I haven't upset any apple carts?'* Once again my heart sank, this is what I was hoping she wouldn't ask *'Oh that's Nancy, she runs a coffee shop in the city, I usually call in on my way to the office I was just asking how she was as she had a bereavement in the family recently'* I answered, hoping that would stop any further questions regarding Nancy.

The rest of the dinner went fine, after that Aimee picked up and the night went on smoothly, the food was incredible, the steak was quite possibly the best I'd ever had in my life, it was cooked to absolute perfection, it tuned out Lobster with all the trimmings was basically Lobster with butter, some kind of sauce and king prawns, I have to admit, it looked delicious. The beers and cocktails went down well and after a small disagreement about how we were going to split the bill, I paid whilst Aimee went to 'Powder her nose'? Whatever that meant, We decided to visit a bar nearby, the drinks flowed and the night went on, before I knew it I looked down at my watch and it was 2am and I was pretty tipsy, Aimee convinced me to try an apple martini, it didn't take much convincing, apple martini's happened to be my guilty pleasure.

Half an hour later we were outside the bar, we'd decided to call it a night and our taxi had just pulled up, we dropped Aimee off first and she gave me a lingering kiss goodnight, she thanked me for the evening and we exchanged numbers, I then got dropped off home, as I walked up the stairs to my apartment I found myself thinking, the whole time I've been in the big city I haven't had 1 girl now all of a sudden I have 2 women vying for my attention, I shook my head and smiled to myself. As I sat on my bed, room spinning ever so slightly I picked up my phone, it now read:

'2 New Messages: Nancy'
Part of me still felt incredibly guilty, although when I saw her tonight I still felt the same way as I did before, I decided to open the messages:

'Hey Lance, Sorry it's been a few days! I really enjoyed drinks the other night, I'm sorry I've been so busy sorting things out with my family, Would you like to meet up again sometime soon? x'

'Hi, It was great to see you tonight Lance, I hope your meeting went well, listen if you're free anytime soon and you'd like to meet up again, let me know :) x'

I decided at this time in the morning and given my current state I opted to leave the texts for now and I'd respond in the morning, as I laid there I couldn't nod off, now that I was alone and it was quiet my mind kept wandering back to what happened to me in the library, who was it? how did they know what I was doing? Is my life potentially in danger? And if so am I endangering both Aimee and Nancy in the process?

Before I knew it, it was morning I looked at the clock 11:43am, my head was a little fuzzy from the night before and I had no idea at what point I eventually nodded off, I grabbed a bottle of water from the fridge and sat down on my sofa, I really need to see Shane again but could I trust him? Before I could go down to the police station there was something I had to do, I grabbed my phone

'Hi Nancy, It was a nice surprise to see you last night, yes I'm free over the next few evenings so please don't hesitate to let me know when you're free and we can meet up if you like? Hopefully our next meeting

wont be quite as brief as last night! x'

I still had no idea what I was going to do about the whole Nancy/
Aimee situation but at the moment I guess we're all just hanging
out, I mean nothing serious is going on with either of them so I
guess for the time being I can see how things go. An hour or so
later I was showered and dressed and heading down to the station,
I wanted to speak to Shane, I didn't know if I could trust him but I
don't have anyone else I can go to, I certainly can't let anyone else
know whats going on and its not like anything could happen to
Shane right? He's a police officer and a pretty respected one at that.

I walked up the stairs into the station and walked up to the front
desk before I could say a word a voice came from a room off to my
left *'Lance? Can't say I expected to see you here again anytime soon'* I
was surprised to see Shane beckoning me into the room, *'Are you
here to see me again?'* I nodded in response, he invited me to take
a seat, as I looked around this was clearly his office, there were
plaques and awards along with front pages in frames on all the
walls, the back wall appeared to be a book shelf filled with various
different books, he offered me a drink and filled me a glass of water
'So.. How can I help today?' I took a sip of water and took a breath, I
still hadn't decided if this was a mistake or not.

I explained everything I'd been doing, I talked about how I was
trying to find some more information about Maurice and how I
wanted to put more backbone to my writing but I was coming up
short and struggling to find anything, I then began to explain my
trip to the library, I was hesitant at first but then it occurred to
me, if I wasn't willing to take this risk and divulge what happened
with Shane, who for some reason deep down, I suspected may be
involved, then just like Quentin said I'd be back doing the stuff
noone else wanted to do, so I told Shane everything.

Once I'd finished, Shane sat there, fingers intertwined infront of
him on the table, he leaned back thoughtfully and didn't say a
word for what felt like an eternity, then he spoke *'Lance, we have*

options, do you want to report this and do you want an investigation into this? Alternatively I can look into this for you outside of an investigation, you have to understand in this job, even when we're done, long done, we still have enemies, I've told you the kind of man Maurice was and how successful he was as a man of the badge, but just because someone gets put away doesn't mean they're there forever you know?' I sat for a moment, if I do this the right way and ask for an investigation then what I'm doing may come out and someone else firstly may steal my story, I couldn't believe this was my first thought, however if I go down the route where Shane investigates for me and he is involved in some way then I'm playing into his hands? I wasn't sure what to do so I went with my gut *'I'd like you to look into this personally for me if you would Shane, if you wouldn't mind?'* he smiled and nodded we exchanged numbers, shook hands and he walked me to the door.

I decided I'd head back to the beginning, I left the station and walked back to the riverside, I sat on one of the many benches near where Maurice's spot was, I was still confused as to why Maurice went from being a police officer to then selling chestnuts by the river? I couldn't help but think it was just like Shane said, even when you leave the force it doesn't mean your past couldn't come back to haunt you, surely Maurice knew that so why would he then decide to sell chestnuts by a river in the same city he worked on the beat in for so many years? Surely he knew there would be a risk him being in the same spot at the same time every day? Something didn't add up and I was angry with myself for not thinking about this until Shane mentioned it, I didn't think Maurice was a foolish man, now I'm thinking is he as innocent as I first thought?

The rest of the day and evening was spent with me sat in my living room pouring over the articles I'd taken from the library with a break every so often to pick up my phone to see if anyone had messaged, nothing, part of me was hoping to hear from Aimee and part of me wanted Nancy to respond, none of me wanted a message from Shane, I thought to myself perhaps Aimee is waiting for me to initiate conversation? Perhaps she's going by first date etiquette and not calling or texting for 48 hours? Was it even a date? I put my phone back down, it was probably a good thing, now isn't the time to be distracted. A couple more hours went by and I was no further than I was when I first started, I looked at my phone again to check the time, 10:56pm, I decided after last nights late night I could use a good nights sleep so I headed off to bed.

I was awoken to the sound of my phone going off on my bed side table, I grabbed it and looked at the name calling, I bolted up right

'Shane Calling'

'Hello?' I answered *'Lance, its Shane, sorry to bother you so early, would you mind coming down to the station? I went down to the library last night and reviewed the CCTV footage, I think you might want to see this'* my entire body filled with dread *'No problem, I'll be down as soon as I can'*

I put down my phone and sank into my bed, I don't think I like where this is going all of sudden.

Chapter Ten

As I laid there staring at my phone, I began to panic, No one knew what I was looking into, no one knew what I was up to so how did anyone first of all know I was at the library and second of all knew what I was looking into? I hadn't told anyone, I hadn't confided in anyone.. Anyone other than Quentin? No my mind very quickly wiped any suspicions about Quentin away, he didn't know the specifics or the ins and outs and he certainly didn't know what I'd been up to, I put my phone down and decided I needed to get to Shane before I lost my nerve.

15 minutes later I found myself in a far too familiar situation, once again I was in the back of a cab on my to a potential lead, only this time I wasn't quite as eager to learn where this one was going to go. As the cab pulled up to the steps at the precinct the nerves began to kick in, I started to feel sick, my palms became sweaty and I all of a sudden became very conscious I needed a drink of water, or something a little stiffer, I handed the driver some money over and muttered for him to keep the change, I climbed out of the cab and began to ascend the stairs, each step feeling heavier and my legs feeling weaker, I opened the door, took one last deep breath and headed into the station.

'Lance, you took your time'

Before I even had chance to get to the desk Shane was already waiting for me, beckoning me into his office, I apologised for my tardiness and made an excuse about waiting for a cab, trying to sound relaxed, I doubt I sounded relaxed in any way. Shane sat down in his seat and offered me a drink, he went to grab the water but must have caught my gaze as he put the water back down and instead grabbed 2 glasses and a bottle of whiskey from his cabinet.

'Lance, I'm sorry if I worried you on my call, but I need you to watch some of this footage with me' he said as he poured out the drinks, he handed a glass to me and tipped his glass as if to cheers, I took a sip and sat down and he pressed play on the monitor in front of us. The screen was relatively dark and slightly grainy, I felt the library could definitely use some new equipment, there were 3 particular camera's we could see: The entrance, The Reception and where I was sat using the computers, we began watching from when I first entered the library from here on Shane put the speed up 3x

'Now Lance, you were in the Library for quite some time, there's something here that is a worry, if we watch the video feed from the entrance, after you, nobody entered the library, people only left which means..'

'Whoever attacked me was already there? I saw my attackers before anything even happened' I completely interjected and finished Shane's sentence off for him

'Exactly, this is what concerns me' he replied, we watched on, he was right, no one entered after me, on the reception feed the tables remained empty throughout my visit, I chill ran down my spine, I didn't like this, not one bit. After what felt like an eternity but was actually more like 20 minutes of video or so, we saw it, as I went over to the printer 2 dark figures grab me from behind, one leaned in and then they let go and were gone, I sat back, I didn't understand why Shane brought me here, he'd found nothing, he had no news and no leads

'Shane? I don't understand?'

'Neither do I, but I watched feed for another hour or so and you're the last person to leave Lance, this means either your attackers didn't use traditionally entrances and exits or they're following you...'

I finished off the whiskey in one, I leant back in my chair, I couldn't get my head around any of this, I took on a story because I had personally met the man and I had no idea of this other side of him? The only thing I could think of now was the old saying 'Curiosity killed the cat' I didn't like how that ended and in this case.. I was the cat.

'Listen, I'm going on a patrol, how about you come with me? Not only will it give you a chance to clear your mind but think about it, if you're being followed and you're getting in a police car do you really think that wouldn't deter any attackers? Thinking you have links in the force?' Shane seemed oddly comforting for once.

I thought for a moment and decided he was right, I agreed to go on the patrol with him, I mean who knows maybe I'll even enjoy myself.

10 minutes later we were stood in a room filled with riot gear, tasers, truncheons and bullet proof vests, one of which Shane passed to me, I looked at him nervously hoping he was going to take it back as a joke

'Don't look so worried, its precaution, look I have to wear one too' Shane said reassuringly.

It wasn't reassuring, I pulled it on and we headed to Shane's car, trying to seem unfazed I pulled out my phone, partially so Shane couldn't see my face and partially because I hadn't checked it since Shane's call.

'2 New Messages: Aimee, Nancy'

Something occurred to me after seeing that *'Shane, If it transpires I am being followed or people are watching me, wouldn't that mean I'm putting people in danger? I mean.. I've seen you a fair few times recently?'* I used Shane as an example to cover up what I was really asking

'Probably, but I'm not worried, I mean who in the right mind would target me?' he retorted, this was not helpful, we climbed into his squad car and set off.

30 minutes later after what felt like a private tour of all the spots Shane's made a big bust we ended up on an industrial estate, Shane pulled on the handbrake and switched off the engine, he climbed out of the car and sat on the bonnet, unsure as to what to do I followed him.

'Remember the story I told you about me and Maurice?'

How could I forget such a tale!? *'I recall the story in question'* I said, he pointed to a factory that was in a relatively poor state *'That's where it all went down...'* I didn't really know how to respond, he seemed so calm but at the same time I could clearly see there was something else going on, I don't know what made me do it or why I thought it was a good idea to go wandering away from Shane, but I headed towards the building, a part of me wanted to see where it all went down, twisted I know, before I got to the door I heard the screech of tires, I spun round as fast I could to see Shane's car speeding off *'Shane?! SHANE!'* I started screaming his name as I sprinted down the street.. Too late he was gone.

Panic set in, here I am, the scene of the crime as it were where Shane and Maurice had their 'run in' I was beginning to feel very sick, my head was spinning, why had he left me? What happened? My legs were weak, I couldn't help but think was Shane behind all this? I mean it wouldn't be hard to see why not, maybe he's had a chip on his shoulder regarding Maurice this whole time? Maybe Shane killed Maurice? My mind was racing at a million miles per hour, it all started to make sense and pieces began to fall in to place.. Maybe this is why the police weren't looking into this, christ.. Here I am, alone, lost and finally think I've got the answer, am I even going to make it anywhere!? I pulled out my phone, frantically began typing out a message with no recipient when all of a sudden the screen went black, my heart sank, I forgot to charge my phone.

I started to run, I didn't know where I was or how to get back to the city, was all of the stories on the way here a rouse to throw me off where we actually were? Damnit Shane.. I couldn't help but let the anger build up, all I could think of was revenge, if I made it out of here I was going to get Shane.. I was going to really get him, as I ran down street after street I had no idea where I was going, I darted down an alley way and the next thing, everything went black.

I opened my eyes, my head was in agony my vision was blurry, someone was stood over me, *'Shane?'* I stammered *'No, Big Sol and you're on my turf kid'* a gruff voice responded, I frantically rubbed my eyes and jumped to my feet, to my surprise a short stocky man stood in front of me, couldn't be bigger than 5'10, 'Big Sol' definitely ironic, I started to mutter an apology and started walking backwards, then I stopped, I couldn't take another step as someone was blocking my way, once again my heart sank, a feeling I'm all too familiar with lately, Big Sol's friends grabbed me whilst Big Sol slipped his hand into his pocket and pulled it out again with a new piece of jewellery, a knuckle duster *'Is this who Shane's working with? It wouldn't surprise me, I had my suspicions he was corrupt from the off'* before I could open my mouth and say a word Big Sol hit me with an uppercut straight to the ribs, all air escaped my body, I definitely heard a crack, I dropped to my *knees 'Why are you here? Who are you?'* I gasped for air *'My name is Dan, I'm not from around here I'm lost and I've taken a wrong turn'* I lied, *'Likely story, seems like a lot of people end up here by accident'* before I knew it kicks and punches were raining down on me, I felt my consciousness slipping away from me, *Was this it? really?*

My body writhing in agony, head pounding, I could feel the blood dripping down my face, all I could see was blue and red flashes, my eyes were beginning to close and the last thing I heard was a gun shot, everything was slow motion, *Suppose I'll never know what ever happened to Maurice, I guess curiosity really did kill the cat.*

Chapter Eleven

I was slipping in and out of consciousness, everything was in slow motion, flashes of moments I seem to recall, opening my eyes seeing blood dripping on the floor I was getting carried along, the next moment I was in the back of a car I could faintly hear someone saying *'Stay with me Lance, don't you dare close your eyes again'* the next time I was on my back, all I could see was bright white lights, I didn't know what was going on, was this it? am I really seeing those bright lights? Is it all over? I tried to take a step towards them but I couldn't feel anything, I couldn't move a muscle, then there was nothing.

I came too and I was in the hospital, I spent the next few days slipping in and out of consciousness, it took 4 or 5 days for me to be fully back compos mentis, after speaking to one of the nurses I was told I'd been beaten to a very dangerous position and if it wasn't for the 'heroic actions' of a police officer I may not have been here, I asked for the name of the officer in question but she didn't know, I was told I'd be in the hospital for another 2 days at least so to get comfortable. During my stay it appears I'd had a few visitors whilst I wasn't quite with it, there was a card on the side from Aimee along side a bottle of whiskey, the gift note on the side simply saying 'See you soon, Q' I couldn't help but wonder how they knew?, I asked the nurse if my phone had been brought back, I was still in no condition to be getting out of bed, deep inhales were agony and the slightest movement almost reduced me to tears, the nurse pulled my phone out of a nearby drawer and handed it to me, luckily there was a spare charger in the lost and found, I plugged my phone in to charge and drifted back off to sleep.

A week had passed and I had finally been told I could leave the hospital that evening, they wanted me to stay until they had chance to give me one last check up to make sure they were happy I could leave, I hadn't had a visitor in the days I'd been awake and even though I charged my phone I'd decided to leave it unchecked, I thought a few days to myself pretending nothing else was going on might do me good, although it didn't quite work out that way, in the lull of the days I'd find myself thinking about everything that happened, why did Shane leave me? Was he working with Big Sol? Who brought me in to the hospital? Once again I was lost in these thoughts when there a nurse came in and interrupted *'Lance? You have a visitor if you're feeling up to it?'* a visitor? I couldn't help but wonder who it was, I nodded and told her I was happy to see them.

What felt like an eternity, despite it was actually only a couple of minutes, the door slid open, I couldn't believe my eyes, fear stricken *'Shane?'* I obviously tried to jump up but quickly collapsed back onto the bed *'Lance, I've come to explain.. Or at least get answers about what happened on the ride along'* what did he mean get answers? Part of me was filled with rage, the rest of me fear, here I was face to face alone in a room with the man who left me to get attacked, he closed the door and took a seat beside me.

Shane started to tell me what happened, he told me he jumped in his car and drove off round the corner, he said he was trying to lighten the mood have a joke and was waiting around the corner for me, he thought I'd be round the corner in a minute as he saw me sprinting after him in his mirror but knew when I never turned the corner something was wrong so he came back down the street and I wasn't there, he said he'd began to panic and began frantically searching the streets when he saw me run through an alley way, by the time he'd got to where I'd ran I was already on the ground with three or four men attacking me, he said he put on his lights, jumped out of his car and fired off a shot into the air, the men then fled and he grabbed me and put me in the back of his car and drove me to the hospital.

I just sat there, all this sounded far too convenient, I mean what kind of a person drives away from someone for a joke? no part of me was now feeling fearful but I was entirely engulfed by rage *'How could you do this to me Shane? Considering what had just happened in the library and now this? Don't you think this is just a little bit too convenient?'* I couldn't even raise my voice so it definitely didn't have the effect I wanted *'Lance, think it through, do you think I'd have contacted your employers to let them know where you were if I did this? I am on YOUR side here, I want to do everything I can to help you get to the bottom of what happened with Maurice'* he stopped and looked at me, I looked back at him and I couldn't help but feel like he was being honest, *'Ok, I give in, I just couldn't understand why you'd do that to me, I thought maybe you had something to do with it, I'm sorry'* I confessed, I guess part of me was upset this had nothing to do with Shane because for a brief moment, I had a lead.

Shane stayed with me for the rest of the afternoon and when the nurse told me I could leave he took me back to my apartment, I'll be honest I still didn't 100% trust Shane but in reality he was my only link to Maurice and considering this latest set back, I'd just lost another week on this case, and In reality I hadn't actually gotten anywhere, I'd decided for now Shane was an ally. It was late into the evening by the time Shane left, once he got me home and inside I offered him a coffee, it was the least I could do since he brought me home and apparently saved my life, so we chatted for a while about Maurice, I didn't give him any specifics about my work and all the files I had and the stuff I'd printed out was hidden from view, I'd decided I'd head to bed once he left, then something occurred to me, whilst I was in the bathroom, admiring my cut and bruised face, I couldn't help but think I looked a little dangerous, I chuckled to myself and instantly regretted it due to pain shooting up my ribs, my first date with Nancy.. I don't know why but I recalled her mentioning a recently deceased uncle?

Surely not? Could it be? Was I really so wrapped up in the whole 'first date' if you could even call it a date, that I blindly overlooked something so key? I walked over to my bed and picked up my phone, there were multiple messages from Nancy I opened them all at once

'19:04 Nancy

It was good to see you tonight Lance, hopefully we'll bump into each other again soon x'

'16:33 Nancy

Hi, Maybe your phone still isn't working? Get back to me if you get this :) x'

11:52 Nancy

Ok, I get it, I don't know what I did but I see when I'm not wanted'

I thought about texting her and telling her everything, but calling would be quicker

'This number is not recognised'

Strange? I tried again

This number is not recognised'

It quickly dawned on me, this wasn't a coincidence, I needed to see Nancy and soon, I looked at the time '22:19' ok I wans't going to be able to see her tonight, I guess tomorrow I'll be getting a coffee, before I went to sleep I thought it was only right to text Aimee.

'Hi Aimee, Thank you for the card, I'm home now, going to rest up for a few days and then I'll be back at work x'

The next morning I woke up and for the first time in a week I felt like I'd had a good nights sleep, no nurses checking up on me in the night, no people screaming throughout the night, I felt like it had done me the world of good, still in pain but well rested, I got up and showered, got dressed and headed for the door, first things first, I need to see Nancy, surely she'd understand my lack of response when she sees me? Hopefully this wasn't wishful thinking.

15 minutes later my cab pulled up outside the coffee shop, I paid my fare and got out, I walked to the door and took a deep breath, as I opened the door and took a step in, the all too familiar warm aromatic air hit me and I couldn't help but smile, I had genuinely missed coming here, luckily it was a mid morning lull and there was noone around, unfortunately I couldn't see Nancy either only the hipster barista, I walked up and I could see him eyeing me up and down, he clearly didn't recognise me, before he could ask me what I wanted, if he was even going to, I asked if Nancy was around, he looked at me sceptically and gave me a sort of grunt and walked off into the back, this was the first time in over a week I'd really walked around unaided and I was immediately feeling it so I headed off to one of the seats.

I'd been sat down for a few minutes when I heard footsteps behind me and truth be told they sounded angry or at least as angry as footsteps can sound, I could tell it was Nancy, as she approached the table I was sat at *'And what exactly can I do for you?'* she said in an angry tone, *'Well..'* I started but as I turned my head to look at her, she gasped and cut me off *'Lance? What happened?'* she said with genuine concern, I invited her to take a seat, she told me to wait and came back 2 minutes later with coffee's, I was glad I somehow avoided a confrontation, I explained the whole story, I told her what had happened, I left out key details such as the library and merely told her Shane was an acquaintance and had invited me on a ride along I naturally used this as my excuse for my ignorance regarding her texts and she said she understood and apologised for the messages she sent.

We sat and spoke for quite some time, it turns out she'd been going through a hard time with her uncles passing, I felt awful because all I could think was hopefully this opens it up to me finding out more about him, all I really knew was he was relatively affluent, she said she didn't really spend too much time with him but and in reality she didn't really know him nor he her but he'd still helped her out financially when she moved to the big city I couldn't help but try swing this in my favour, I asked had she visited his grave since he passed away and she told me she hadn't, she said she didn't want to go alone, so I went for it

'Do you want to go? With me? I'm happy to accompany you, although we'll have to take it easy'

She looked at me for a moment and then said *'I'd like that'*

And just like that, the door was open, 20 minutes later we were in a cab talking and joking like we were before I met Aimee, part of me missed this, I genuinely felt me and Nancy could or at least could have had something. We got out of the cab and started walking up to the grave, I never really liked visiting graveyards I couldn't help but feel slightly unnerved, I don't know why, they just gave me the creeps, we followed the path down and headed towards a large oak tree in the distance, the grave was under there, around 10 feet away from where we were going, she stopped, she took a deep breath and locked into my arm tight and began walking again, we stopped and she knelt down beside a grave I heard her starting to sob, I could tell she was trying to hide it so I knelt beside her and put my arm around her, I glanced over at the grave, my heart sank.

'Jacob Adams
1948-2019
RIP'

I knew it was too good to be true, once again, the trail goes cold.

Chapter Twelve

As I sat there with my arm around Nancy as she silently wept I couldn't help but feel disappointed, I really thought I had something, it seems every avenue I turn down is a dead end and I keep coming up short. I was lost in thought for a few minutes before Nancy turned and buried her head in my shoulder which quickly brought me back around, I put my arm around her and stood up, she wiped away the tears and told me they weren't overly close however she couldn't help but feel such sadness for her loss, I comforted her and hailed a cab, selfishly being annoyed the whole time, I helped her into the cab and climbed in afterwards, heading back to the coffee shop I couldn't help but stew, Nancy thankfully assumed I was leaving her to her own thoughts.

We arrived back a little while later, being the gentleman as always, I helped Nancy out of the cab and held the door open for her, which was clearly a good move as she started to smile again, which did briefly take my mind off what had happened at the graveyard, *briefly,* we sat down in a quiet corner and Nancy brought over 2 coffee's, I had to admit, I'd missed the coffee and the fleeting moments with Nancy, we talked for a while and she thanked me for accompanying her, she had wanted to go for a while but couldn't face going alone, honestly, having Nancy open up a little was nice, for a change I wasn't focused on what had happened to Maurice and I felt like we having a genuine connection, an hour or two passed in what felt like the blink of an eye, before I knew it the store was closing.

Nancy had invited me to stay a little longer, but I made my excuses and left, as much as I wanted to stay there were things I needed to do and in all honesty there was a nagging in the back of my mind that was telling me not to get too close to Nancy.. Well anyone really, I was already worried about my own safety so I didn't really want to put anyone else in any danger. After I left the coffee shop I headed to work, I hadn't been in the office for some time and thought I better show my face as I'd pretty much neglected everything other than my story, part of me was thankful I was even still getting a paycheque. A short while later I found myself back in the elevator heading up to floor 45, hoping Quentin hadn't gone home, the doors opened and I headed down that familiar corridor, Aimee wasn't at her desk, I couldn't help feel a little sad at that, I walked up to Quentin's office and knocked.

'Come in'

I opened the door and poked my head through, Quentin had his phone to his ear and was seemingly in a pretty heated discussion, I couldn't help but feel I'd walked in at a bad time but he gave a wave and gestured me to sit down, I headed over and took my seat, I couldn't help but feel I had nothing but happy memories in this office, all of them on the otherside of the desk. Quentin wrapped up his call and offered me a drink, I was happy with water today, my head was still a little fragile so I decided to give the liquor a miss

'Lance, good to see you up and well, How're you feeling?' asked Quentin, sounding a little like a concerned father *'I'm feeling much better now, I actually came to thank you for the gift you sent whilst I was in hospital'* Quentin then asked me what had happened and how I ended up in hospital, I told him a slightly different story cutting out a few details, I explained I'd just been walking through a bad neighbourhood to clear my head but didn't realise it was bad until it was too late, he bought it *'You're lucky that officer came by, who knows what might've happened had he not'* I agreed, our conversation continued for a few more minutes, just casual chat, then suddenly Quentin stood up, Whiskey in hand

and walked over to the window overlooking his office *'Lance, I hate to ask but, well I haven't heard from you in a while about this case? What's going on? I appreciate its your first 'big' case but he was just a chestnut vendor and the death has been chalked off as not suspicious?'* I panicked *'It's coming along really well, I'll be honest, I'm sorry I'm dragging my heels a little but as you say its my first 'big' case and I really want it to show that I'm a good journalist, I can have a rough draft for you in a couple of days if you like?'* I lied and this wasn't a good lie, in reality I had nothing, I was no further on from when I barged into his office demanding this case promising big things *'No, Don't worry about it, you've just got out of hospital, I'm sure I can wait for the final piece'* he responded, I couldn't believe my luck, I needed to make my excuses and leave before I made anymore promises I can't deliver on *'Ok Quentin, thank you, I'll get it to you asap, I'm sorry I came up without an appointment I was just worried I hadn't been around for a while, I'll get out of your way and let you get back to what you were doing, I've probably overdone it today anyway'* I lied, again, I got up and left, as I closed the door behind me I couldn't help but feel bad about lying to Quentin, afterall he's the one that's given me this opportunity, although now I couldn't help but wish he hadn't.

'Hello stranger'

I looked up *'Aimee'* the words kind of fell out of my mouth, Aimee looked stunning as always, she walked over and put her hand gently on my face, I couldn't help but feel my heart rate increase and my knee's feel weak *'Look at you, your face is a mess, I came to see you at the hospital but you were asleep and I didn't want to bother you'* I was shocked she came, although now I think about it, who else would've come and dropped off the card off if not Aimee *'I.. '* before I could say anything she cut me off *'Why don't you come over later? I'll be finished here around 9'* I stared in disbelief, was Aimee suggesting what I thought she was? I couldn't help but think I'd be a fool to turn her down *'Meet you outside at 9 then?'* I tried to sound cool and nonchalant about it but I'm pretty confident Aimee saw through it, she smiled and said *'see you at 9, Don't eat'* and she walked into Quentin's office and I headed home.

9pm soon rolled around and I was stood outside work, I almost didn't make it, I spent 20 minutes packing an overnight bag and heading out of the door before realising how presumptuous that was and ran back inside to leave it, I mean she never mentioned staying over and imagine the embarrassment of turning up with a bag and her asking me to leave, I stood there for a good 10 minutes before Aimee emerged just as a cab pulled up, she linked my arm and lead me to the cab, I couldn't help but think this was all backwards, she was so cool and sophisticated about all of this and I was just along for the ride. Eventually we arrived at Aimee's building, a block of nice modern apartments a far cry from the modest apartments in my building, Aimee was on the top floor, she led me into her apartment and told me to make myself comfortable whilst she got us a drink, I walked over to the window and the view was breath taking, I could see all across the city, in all the years I've lived here the only view I'd ever had that compared to this was, well.. Last time I was with Aimee, I couldn't help but think Aimee had a thing for views, just as my mind began to wander she came back over and handed me a drink.

Aimee had already ordered pizza's and they had arrived shortly after we did, I couldn't help but be quietly impressed she had some with pineapple on, something I was a fan of and clearly as was she, as the night wore on and the drinks flowed, the conversation turned to work *'I'm looking forward to reading your piece you know, Quentin expects big things from you'* the drink had slightly elevated my confidence *'You know Aimee, he might just be right, I'm hoping this story is a big break for me'* she smiled at me and agreed *'do I get a sneak peak then before you release it?'* she asked *'I'm not sure it'll be too interesting, its just about an old Chestnut seller'* I tried to make it sound uninteresting *'Wait, the one who used to be down by the river? I've been wondering where he went'* she sounded interested, I definitely didn't want to give any information away *'Ah well, All shall be revealed, I wouldn't want to ruin the surprise'* I said whilst giving her a smile and a wink *'You know Lance, you do have an edge of mystery about you'* she moved closer and whispered in my ear *'I like it'*

Before I knew it Aimee was kissing my neck and unbuttoning my shirt, I couldn't believe what was happening, she began kissing down my body and pulled off my belt, I pulled her up and started kissing her, slowly moving down to kissing her neck, she pushed me off I looked at her startled and she grabbed my arm and dragged me off into her bedroom, infront of me saw a big four poster bed, she pulled me towards it and pushed me down she started kissing me again and then stood up *'Get comfortable, I'll be right back'* I didn't need to be told twice, I quickly got undressed and laid back on the bed, I couldn't believe my luck. After a couple of minutes the door opened again, Aimee was stood there in some silky lingerie and I could not believe my eyes I sat up and she walked over she pushed me back down and climbed on top of me, kissing me all over, she was being extra gentle around the bruises all over my ribs and body, I felt so relaxed, then I remembered how she took control last time, I rolled her over and started kissing down her body I undid the lingerie she was wearing and she threw it off to the side her hands were all over, her nails digging into my back, I could feel them digging into my skin as she dragged her hands down, she was biting my ears breathing heavily, I was whispering sweet nothings in her ear and she was loving every second of it, she bit into my shoulder and I could feel her bite getting firmer, then she let out a gasp and collapsed backwards with me on top of her. I rolled off her to the side, I was out of breath she turned to face me and kissed me again, I smiled and went off to the bathroom, as I was splashing my face with water to cool down I noticed Aimee's phone on the side of the sink

'2 Missed Calls: Unknown Number'

I thought it was strange, I mean who takes their phone into the bathroom? But after that I didn't give it a second thought, we all have quirks, I went back to bed, I climbed in next to Aimee and put my arm around her, she put her head on my chest and we both fell asleep.

I woke up in the morning alone in bed, there was a note next to me *'Lance, had to go to work, the keys are by the door'* I laid for a moment and reflected on the night before, I couldn't help but smile, I got up showered and got dressed, I grabbed Aimee's keys and headed to the office, I'd decided it was time to get to the bottom of this whole Maurice scenario, I dropped the keys off at Aimee's desk, she wasn't around so I decided to head back to the one place I knew would be able to get some answers, I headed back to Shane's office.

As I stood at the foot of the stairs to the precinct, I knew I really didn't want to be here, but I had nowhere else to turn, so I went to the door and took a deep breath, I pushed the door and walked inside heading towards the receptionist

'Cant keep away can you Lance?'

I turned around and Shane was already beckoning me into his office, I walked in and sat down *'How did you know I was coming?'* he smiled and pointed at his screen showing the CCTV, I apologised for my hastiness, *'Well then, I'll be honest I didn't expect to see you here anytime soon, what can I do for you?'* he asked *'Can I see the files on Maurice's death? Or at least ask some details'* I asked hopefully, knowing the outcome already *'I can't do that Lance, they're private files, the case is closed so I wouldn't really have access to them'* I already knew that was coming *'Shane, you've seen the tape at the library, something is obviously going on here and I want to find out what seeing as my life feels like its in danger, I feel I have a right to know, do I have to file a formal enquiry? Because I will if I have to'* I tried sounding as stern as possible *'Ok, fair enough, its up to you, I'll give you two options, option 1 you file an official report and we go down that route no problem, Option 2 we'll deal with this, just me and you'* I sat for a moment and thought about it, I mean, Shane already knows where I live and all my personal information so no matter what the situation, he can know where I am at all times and I suppose the less people that know the better *'Ok, Option 2'* he smiled, which worried me as there was still something I didn't quite trust about him, *'I thought you might say that'* I looked at him and he got up and walked to his door *'Come on, we're going for another ride'*

Considering how the last ride I took with Shane turned out, I wasn't thrilled to be hearing those words again, but what other choice did I have?

Chapter Thirteen

Here I was once again sat in a car heading to an unknown destination with Shane, I couldn't help but feel this was definitely a situation I didn't want to find myself in again anytime soon but unfortunately due to circumstance, this was unavoidable. We spent the first part of the journey in relative silence, I was still feeling pretty uneasy about everything when Shane finally spoke *'So we've been in the car for a while now and you haven't even asked where we're heading'* it then dawned on me I hadn't and it hadn't even crossed my mind *'I thought it might be an interesting surprise, but I suppose if you want to tell me..'* I joked, hoping I didn't come across as nervous as I felt, he looked over at me and smiled *'We're heading to Maurice's house'* I acted as nonchalant as I could, but I was feeling a mixture of emotions, elation and happiness at the fact I could possibly, finally make some headway but at the same time worry and nervousness, considering what happened last time I couldn't help but wonder if I was being set up?

Eventually we pulled up to a large estate, it felt like we'd been driving for hours, although we couldn't have been more than a mile or two outside the city, I couldn't help but look up at the estate in front of me, I couldn't believe the older gentleman I saw every morning selling chestnuts by the river lived here, then it dawned on me, he wasn't exactly *just* a chestnut vendor, but that was part of the problem, just who was Maurice Caspian? I was lost in this thought when Shane cleared his throat *'You ready Lance?'* I nodded and went to climb out of the car *'Erm Lance?'* I looked over at Shane *'So, this is strictly off the record and well, we're not exactly supposed to be here nor do we have any sort of clearance to be here so I'm going to have to ask you to leave your phone in the car if you don't mind'* He looked serious, I felt my palms getting sweaty and I took a moment to answer, I contemplated my options, I mean now I know where he lives, I could just ask to turn around and go home and come back later on my own, although I'm sure Shane had already taken all this into account, I had no choice *'I understand'* I said as I put my phone in the glove compartment, we climbed out of the car and walked up to the gates, here we go.

As we walked up to the gates Shane stopped and pulled something out of his *pocket 'Put these on'* and handed me a pair of latex gloves, I looked at him surprised and he answered the question before it even came out *'We cant leave any evidence of us being here, as I said this isn't exactly on the record'* I nodded and we put on the gloves, he pushed open the gates and we continued up a tree lined path lit by small lamps, I had so many questions running through my mind, I mean, surely a police officer, no matter how good they were or how well thought of they were, no way would they be able to afford a place like this, would they? *'Shane? How exactly did Maurice afford a place like this?'* the words sort of just fell out of my mouth, I didn't intend on asking *'I'd like to know that myself Lance'* his answer was cold and I could tell I didn't want to push this line of questioning any further. We came to the front door and I couldn't help but be surprised at the amount of security that was around, Shane had already explained all the surveillance gear I was seeing had been turned off as all the tapes had been removed and were being held down at the precinct, there were camera's everywhere, Shane took out a key and opened the door, I braced myself and stepped over the threshold.

Shane flicked a switch by the door and turned on all the lights, at this point it was pretty clear to me this wasn't Shane's first time here, I looked around and we were in the main foyer in front of me was a large staircase leading up to the second floor, the foyer was covered in white marble, walls were adorned by abstract art and unusual hangings, it seemed Maurice had quite an eclectic taste when it came to art, *'Lance, stick with me, I don't want you getting separated from me in here, we're only sticking to the ground floor ok?'* Shane said sternly, I couldn't help but wonder why he was putting such strict rules on our visit but I agreed nonetheless. We walked to the left of the staircase which led into a large room, again marble flooring, I guessed this was going to continue throughout, there was a bookcase on the far wall full of books and boxes, I walked over and opened one of the boxes, nothing but small trinkets, nothing particularly outstanding so I closed it and put I back, nothing was making sense, first of all why would anyone do anything to Maurice? Secondly and more unusual, why would there be no investigation into a former police officers death?

We continued through the house, the first room was minimalistic, if anything it seemed like things had been removed, other than the book case and a few more pieces of unusual art there wasn't much in there a chair, a table and a television set, the next room we came to was a dining area with a long table and several seats around it, the places were still set, it was as if someone had a dinner party arranged, it was a strange set up, I couldn't help but feel this house appeared to be still being lived in, Shane was oddly silent, I didn't question this I was taking in my surroundings. I stopped in the doorway of the dining room, something was bothering me, nothing seemed out of place, no signs of a break in, but something didn't feel right, before I had too much chance to dwell on these thoughts Shane broke his silence *'Lance, come on, we're not staying long'* I didn't have much choice if I wanted to see more, the next room we came to was the kitchen, it was almost surgically clean, it looked like none of the utensils had ever even been used, ideally I'd be able to take pictures on my phone but I couldn't, I appreciated why Shane asked me to leave my phone but I wish I hadn't.

The next room was finally something a little different, there was a pool table, globe, dart board and in the corner, Maurice's chestnut cart, I didn't want to seem too eager so I panned around the room looking at the globe and gave it a small spin I approached the pool cues and admired them, even though I knew very little about pool I then walked past the edge of the pool table, it was then I noticed something strange, the rest of the house thus far was pretty pristine and well kept however I couldn't help but notice a few scuff marks on the cloth, I made a mental note to write this down later. I walked over to the chestnut cart and I took my time inspecting it, this clearly aroused Shane's suspicion because for the first time since entering the house he engaged in conversation, however it was in a low hushed voice which I found strange *'You seem to have quite an interest in this Lance?'* he questioned, without hesitation I responded *'An old friend of mine had one similar to this, I haven't seen one in ages, strange place to keep one though, surely it gets in the way'* I reached to open the side but before I could Shane grabbed my hand and put his finger to his mouth and looked up, I followed his gaze, footsteps, he grabbed me and pulled me close to him *'Do not make a sound'* he was serious, I began to panic but I knew I needed to keep calm, my breathing got heavy and I began to feel light headed.

Shane grabbed my wrist and pulled me quietly to an alcove under the stairs, *Shane had definitely been here before, how did he know all these hiding spots?* I didn't have time to process anything, I could hear voices and footsteps, they were getting louder, I was about to ask Shane how we were going to get out of here but before I could open my mouth he spun round and put his palm firmly over my mouth, he looked worried, if Shane was worried then I was definitely worried. A few minutes passed and the voices and steps got louder, they were directly above us now, Shane pulled me down so we were crouched in a corner, there were at least 3 or 4 people in the house with us, they were coming down the stairs, my heart was racing, they were getting closer and closer, I was trying to control my breathing but I was struggling, I saw Shane put one hand on his gun and the other to his face with his finger over his mouth, the people were mere feet away from us.

The people were taking I was in a state of panic and I couldn't even hear what they were saying, I could see them, I couldn't make them out and I couldn't say what they looked like but there were 4 visible figures, I heard one of them question why the lights were on but they shrugged it off they were getting closer and closer, panic was well and truly starting to set in, what were we going to do? And then it happened, they reached the alcove we were hidden in, for a moment I felt time stand still, I was very aware of every breath I took, even my blinks sounded like gun shots to me, I could feel every beat of my heart, and just like that, *they walked right by*, straight into the games room we had been in moments before, I looked at Shane, fear stricken, we heard them rolling the balls out onto the table and laughing. Shane grabbed my arm again and pulled me towards the door, I couldn't help but be impressed with him, he grabbed the handle and waited for the perfect moment the balls clattered together and used the sound to cover our escape he pulled me off the path and away from the lights I opened my mouth to speak and he just shook his head and I didn't say a word, we ran down through the trees and out of the gate, we ran across the road and got back in Shanes car, he looked at me and said *'Ok Lance, there might be something I've not been entirely truthful about'* I looked at him in disbelief.

I knew it!

Chapter Fourteen

As I sat there looking on at Shane expectantly waiting for some big revelation *'Well?'* I asked, Shane looked over at me and said *'Now's not the time or place, we're heading back to town, I'll drop you at your building and then wait for me call'* I looked on in disbelief, surely he didn't just say what I thought he said *'Sorry?'* he looked at me in a way that told me not to ask anymore questions without saying a word *'Look I know you're disappointed Lance but lets be honest, you haven't been open with me either have you? I know you're a reporter and this is probably just another scoop to you and you have zero interest in Maurice himself, you can wait for answers, you'll get them but you'll get them when I call you'* I looked at him and then sat back in my chair *'Ok Shane, I'll wait for the call'* I spent the majority of the journey back gazing out of the window, wondering what Shane was hiding.

By the time we finally pulled up to my building my head was pounding, not only from Shane's revelation but also everything that had happened at Maurice's place, on top of that Shane had obviously done some investigating into me which was a bit worrying but in fairness expected of a police officer, without really saying a word I sort of mumbled a good bye of sorts to Shane grabbed my phone and climbed out of his car, I headed up to my apartment trying to decide on my next steps. I walked through the door and slumped on my sofa, I grabbed a pad and quickly scribbled as much down about the events that unfolded today, I spent over an hour writing everything down and trying to remember every tiny detail but something was still niggling in the back of my mind and I couldn't figure out what, I pulled out everything I had on Maurice and started to pour over all the pages and pages I had and then it hit me, I scrambled through to find the original article and there it clearly said *'Local millionaire found dead in his penthouse'* Penthouse? But today I went to Maurice's *House?* Something didn't add up, I initially took no notice of the headline and was too focused on Maurice being a millionaire, I needed help, but I had no one to turn to, I decided to sleep on it.

I was awoken by the sun blazing through my window, I grabbed my phone to check the time 09:16, I jumped in the shower, had a quick shave, threw on some clothes and sat on the edge of my bed phone in hand scrolling through my contacts, who could I turn to? Who could help me, no names were jumping out at me and even if they did, I couldn't help but wonder if I'd be putting them in danger by talking to them? What choice did I have?

'Hey, Can you meet by the river in an hour? x'

I'd sent it, I'd made my decision and now I had to deal with the consequences, if there were any, maybe I was being over dramatic, chances are everything is going to be fine.

'Hey Lance, Sure I'll see you there in an hour x'

I grabbed my bag and gathered up all the important stuff I thought I'd need, the original article, the article about Maurice after the incident with Shane, the notes I'd taken at the house and threw them all in my bag, I'd decided I was going to walk to the river the fresh air would do me good. It took me a good 45 minutes to walk to the bench beside the river where I used to see Maurice every morning, I was still feeling some of the after affects from the beating given to me by Big Sol, I sat there on the bench looking out at the water, feeling a little bit sorry for myself and wondering where I was going to go from here, the way I saw it I had 3 options, I could carry on and get to the bottom of this, I could drop it, forget the article and go back to the mundane boring day to day stuff I was doing before and hope for no repercussions or I could back home, *home home,* before I even came to the city, before I could dwell on those thoughts too much, my thought process was cut.

'Earth to Lance?'

I must've been zoning out staring across the river without even realising.

'Nancy! Thank you for coming at such short notice, I didn't know if you'd be free'

Nancy handed me a coffee and smiled *'The usual'* I smiled, wrapped my hands around the cup, gave it a gentle blow and took a sip *'Perfect as always'* Nancy smiled and sat down beside me *'So Lance, I didn't expect to hear from you this morning?'* I looked at her and for a moment I didn't say a word, was I really about to do this? Do I really want to get Nancy involved? No I didn't but I could trust Nancy, she was a smart, kind, beautiful woman and by asking her to meet me here today I'd already made the decision, I told her everything, well almost everything, I didn't include Aimee. 10 minutes went by, not a word, we sat there in silence, I'd told Nancy everything about Maurice, Shane, the attack at the library, Maurice's house, then Nancy took a deep breath and finally broke the *silence 'Ok I guess you've had a lot going on, I suppose I forgive you for being so hot and cold'* she joked, I smiled back at her, the last few weeks have been so serious it was refreshing *'Well, I'm not sure how much help I can be but I'd be happy to help in any way I can? Or any way you think I can?'* I was relieved to hear those words, this was the perfect opportunity for Nancy to walk away from me and considering how I'd treat her, I wouldn't have blamed her.

We headed back to the coffee shop and Nancy closed it up for the day, she drew the blinds and locked the door, she brought out her laptop and replenished our drinks *'Right, Ok Lance, here's what we're going to do, all those articles you've got and everything you've wrote down, I'm going to catch up on it all, I'll read all those and see if I find anything and you are going to man the laptop, now you've already dug into Maurice's past and didn't come up with too much but what about this Shane character? You said you didn't trust him? What about seeing if there's anything about him?'* I was taken aback,

I hadn't seen this side of Nancy before, she was commanding and knew exactly what to do, I agreed she was right and pulled the laptop over to me, it was going to be a long day. Over the next few hours Nancy was reading in silence catching up on everything I'd found and searched whilst I was combing old articles for Shane, I wasn't having much luck and decided we needed a break, I ordered in some food and asked Nancy what was going on with her, we chatted for a while about nothing mostly, since our trip to the graveyard Nancy had been back and tidied up the grave, she told me it had been much easier to go back after the initial trip we took, I couldn't help but feel good about helping her get over that first hurdle, mid conversation our food finally turned up, I hadn't realised before but I was starving.

We polished off our food and I took away the cutlery and sat back down, Nancy suggested we swapped so I could go back through my stuff and see if anything came back to me I may have missed, I agreed I thought that was a good idea, plus I was tired of reading about how much of a 'good guy' Shane was, I don't get it, I don't know why but there was something about Shane I just couldn't put my finger on, he gave me no reason to believe he wasn't helping me but at the same time some of the things that happened I couldn't help but not trust him. Another hour or two passed by and things had stopped going in, I was no longer taking anything in I was just staring at the pages not even able to read them, Nancy was scribbling away on a piece of paper and she had been for some time, she was concentrating hard and I didn't want to interrupt. Eventually Nancy finished, closed her laptop leaned back and let out a sigh *'Ok Lance, I think we should leave it there for now, we're not getting anywhere fast and its getting late'* I agreed *'Before I go, Nancy, do you want to go for a walk down by the river? I just want to go back to Maurice's spot again'* she smiled and said *'I guess it makes more sense we walked there on our first date, but yes lets go'* she got up and put her belongings away I thought to myself *'Did she say date?'* I packed up all my papers and put on my coat and bag, we headed out the door and down to the river.

We walked for a while laughing and joking, Nancy wrapped around my arm the whole time, there were moments I forgot why we were even walking around the river and considered asking if she wanted to come back to my place and open a bottle of wine, I didn't even drink wine, I'd just seen it in the movies. We got back to the bench and sat down, I put my arm around Nancy and I told her the exact spot Maurice was in every morning and how we greeted each other and even occasionally had a short chat and I never had any idea who he was, mid conversation the atmosphere was ruined by loud police sirens, I turned my head and saw a patrol car slowly going past, I couldn't help but feel my heart begin to race, I all of a sudden got very nervous, surely that wasn't who I thought it was, I grabbed Nancy's hand *'Come on lets go'* trying my best to stay calm and not sound nervous, we walked down the path and towards the cabs which congregated in a nearby car park, I flagged down a car for Nancy, she turned to me and said *'I'll help you get to the bottom of this Lance, don't worry'* she kissed me on the cheek and got into the cab, I smiled and watched them drive off, I flagged my own cab and headed home.

20 minutes later I was walking through my door, I put down my bag and took off my coat I slumped back down onto my sofa and let out a big exhale, I was hoping the old proverb *a problem shared is a problem halved* could ring true for me, I wasn't hopeful. I'd decided I'd had a long day and I was beat, I took myself off to bed and lay there, wide awake for what felt like hours, everything that had happened to me swirling around in my mind, nothing was making sense, there were no clear connections and there was something I was missing, it was right there but I couldn't see it, I just couldn't put my finger on it, I was in for a long night.

I was awoken abruptly, I could hear a banging and it sounded close, I looked at the time on my phone 04:52, who was even around at this time? I sat up and the noise was getting louder, I got up out of bed and headed to my lounge, the noise had suddenly stopped, the stairs in my building were notoriously loud but it seems whoever was out there had found what they were looking for, I heard the floorboards on my hall start to squeak, my room was only lit by the light coming in through the window from the street, I stood perfectly still trying to be as quiet as possible and then I saw it, an envelope slipped through my door, I tiptoed over as quick and as quietly as I could and looked through my spyhole all I could see was a hooded figure heading down the stairs, this time as quiet as a mouse, they wanted to be heard.

I picked up the envelope and slowly opened it, did I really want to see what was inside? My fingers trembling I slowly pulled out the contents of the envelope, I looked down and my heart sank, the all too familiar feeling of guilt and regret washed over my body, I knew I'd messed up.

Chapter Fifteen

As I sat slumped on my sofa, I leaned forward and grabbed the envelope again, I pulled out the contents to examine them once more, pictures of me and Nancy, pictures of me and Aimee and pictures of me and Shane all from different times and all of them complete unnoticed, someone has been following me, someone knows something and they're worried, now I was worried. Hours passed and all I did was pace the room trying to piece things together, nothing added up and nothing made sense, what exactly was going on? I glanced down at my phone 07:31 I was a mess, I'd barely slept, I was nervous and I felt disgusting, I decided the best thing to do would be shower and then go see Nancy see if she could make sense of any of this.

30 minutes later I was out of the shower, dry and dressed, I decided to text Nancy to make sure she was free

'Hey, Are you free this morning? x'

I decided I'd try tidy the apartment a little whilst I waited for a response, in reality I think I was trying anything to keep my mind off the envelope. I was mid way through tidying my bedroom around 15 minutes later when my phone went off

'1 New Message: Shane'

'Are you free today? Need to speak to you. Shane.'

This was not the text I was anticipating and frankly at the moment, one I really didn't need although I guess I could kill 2 birds with 1 stone, I responded

'Hey Shane, yes I'm free today, there's also something I'd like to speak to you about too, do you have a time and place in mind?'

The response was almost instantaneous

'1 New Message: Shane'

'Yes, Meet me at the diner 2 blocks from your office in an hour, Shane.'

An hour? Seemed kind of ominous but I guess the sooner I see him the better, I quickly finished what I was doing and grabbed my coat, I stuffed the envelope along with a few other pieces of information into my bag and set off, I knew which diner he meant, I'd once called in for breakfast on my way to one the hundreds of mundane dog shows I attended, as I recall the pancakes were incredible and my stomach was rumbling.

As I opened the door to the diner the smell of food filled my nostrils, I was hoping Shane hadn't arrived yet so I could order some breakfast before he got there, I glanced around hopefully but unfortunately saw him beckoning me over from the far corner, I tried to hide the disappointment as I walked over and sat down. A waitress came over and asked if she could get us anything, Shane just ordered a strong coffee whereas I couldn't help myself I ordered a coffee and pancakes, as soon as the words left my mouth I felt Shane's eyes burning into the side of my face, the waitress walked off and Shane gave me a look.

We sat in silence for a while, I didn't know how to open the conversation and Shane seemed unwilling, our coffee's came and I sat quietly eating my pancakes, they were just as delicious as I remember, perfectly fluffy and covered in maple syrup, I was a big kid at heart when it came to pancakes, once I'd finished Shane looked at me and finally said something *'Now you're finished we can get on with what we need to discuss'* I wiped my mouth and I looked at him *'Shane, what exactly haven't you been telling me?'* he looked at me and took a drink of his coffee, he sighed and then he started to talk

'Lance, you said it yourself, a former officer dies and noone bats an eyelid? Well I thought the same, and I'd been doing some digging before you turned up at the precinct, I told you before, Me and Maurice were on the beat together, but we weren't together forever, eventually our paths led away from each other and we went our separate ways, we stayed in touch for a while but you know how it is, work is work and eventually you sort of stop hearing from each other, I didn't hear from Maurice for sometime and then around 5 years ago I was invited to his retirement, Maurice wasn't quite at retirement age so I thought it was strange, but sometimes in this line of work you don't always make it so I went along and everything was normal, it was a nice evening, we spoke briefly and I told him I wouldn't be the officer I was today without him, he shook my hand and told me he was proud of me and that was that, then after a while there were rumours he didn't retire, more like he was forced out, there were rumblings that Maurice wasn't quite as straight laced and by the book as he used to be and someone had found out but due to his record they decided it was time for him to 'retire' rather than leave, I refused to believe this and it was forgotten about pretty quickly, then all this happened and you turned up, Lance I think those rumours may have been true, I think Maurice had something else going on'

I sat there, reeling from what he had said, I was confused, the way Shane said it initially I was ready for some big revelation on how he was in on it and Maurice's death was some big cover up, I was disappointed and relieved, I was happy now as I didn't feel my life was in danger with Shane.. However this information was nothing, it gave me nothing, I was still nowhere and in all honesty I was starting to really feel the pressure from Quentin, despite him never actually putting any on me, I was in a strange situation.

'Well..?' Shane looked at me expecting an answer, I must've been quiet for longer than I thought so I looked at him for a moment and I pulled the envelope out of my bag

'Funny you should say that Shane, because I think you're right,

Maurice definitely isn't the man we thought he was because well.. Look' I slid him the envelope and he opened it up *'And the ladies? Lance I didn't have you down as the type'* I was taken aback, I think this is the first time I'd heard Shane being anything other than stone cold serious *'Well either way, we're in this together now Lance, whoever has sent these pictures clearly has it in for whoever is in them and doesn't want something getting out, but what? What could Maurice possibly have been involved in? Lance do you have a copy of these?'* I looked at him and reactively put my hands on the top of the pictures *'Sorry Shane I don't, but I could get a copy and run them over for you this afternoon?'* he looked at me thoughtfully *'Hmm, No, come down to the station, I'll take a copy of them there and then Lance you've got a job to do, I don't know who these ladies are but you need to speak to them, you need to tell them they could quite possibly be in danger'* I looked at him and knew he was right, I grudgingly agreed to head to the station.

We got to the station and Shane took copies of all the pictures he gave me the originals back and told me to go speak to Nancy and Aimee, he was right, they deserved to know about what was going on, however there was one slight issue, I'd decided to separate the pictures, I moved the ones of me and Aimee to a back pocket in my bag and kept the ones of me and Nancy in the envelope, I was trying to decide who to speak to first when fate intervened.

'Lance? What've you been up to then?'

I looked up and saw Aimee walking towards me smiling, I was confused for a moment and then realised she probably just watched me walk out of the precinct stuffing papers into my bag, I guess it could look like something it wasn't very easily, I smiled back and just told her it was something to do with the case I was looking into *'Listen Aimee, I'm glad I bumped into you, are you free? I need to speak to you about something'* she looked at me apologetically and said *'Sorry Lance, I'm just* running *an errand but we can catch up soon ok?'* and with that she kissed me on the cheek and walked off, *Well, I tried.*

I pulled out my phone to check the time and was relived

'1 New message: Nancy'

Perfect, hopefully Nancy is free, I opened the message 'Hey Lance, I'm free this evening around 8ish if that's ok? x' I responded immediately 'Sure, see you at 8 outside the coffee shop x' I'd decided meeting in the busy street was the best way to go, hopefully we could disappear into the crowd, I couldn't help but be nervous and keep glancing around, just incase I was being followed again, I mean, I was obviously being followed and now I was alone it really hit home that I'm pretty vulnerable, I decided to head straight home and maybe try have a nap as I was running on empty.

I'd flagged down a cab at the precinct and came home, I had him drop me around the corner where it was quiet so I could walk the 2 minutes to my building and look around, I felt if someone was following me, getting dropped somewhere so quiet I would be able to notice someone or something strange lurking around, however there was nothing, I ran up the stairs in my building, feeling like a child again turning off a light and sprinting up the stairs to my bedroom without looking back, feeling like I was being chased, I opened my door and locked it behind me, I drew all the curtains and set my alarm for 6pm, I climbed in bed and forced myself into an uneasy sleep.

I was awoken by my alarm, feeling groggy and a little worse for where I sat up, I grabbed the glass of water I had beside my bed and took a drink, I decided another shower was in order before meeting Nancy, I showered and dried off and pulled out some of my nicer clothes, I didn't know why I was making such an effort considering the situation, I just felt like for Nancy, I wanted to look my best, I pottered around and tried to piece together what I was going to say before I knew it 7pm had rolled around and I'd decided to walk this time, I grabbed my coat, fastened it up and grabbed the envelope, I went outside my building, turned up my collar and set off into the city.

Maybe fresh air was what I needed, this walk felt like it was really doing me good, my mind was clearing, my nerves though shot, felt better, I felt relaxed and like for a moment, everything was ok, however all this was dashed in an instant as a car went screeching past, my heart went into overdrive and once again I turned up the collar on my coat, put my head down and carried on, full steam ahead. I was around 10 minutes away from the coffee shop, I checked my phone 19:38, perfect I was going to be there nice and early which is what I always preferred, I was always nervous of having people wait around for me, I rounded the corner and then stopped, 3 figures were stood in front of me, I froze, one of them looked at me then looked to the side at a car and muttered *'get in'* I wasn't in a position to argue I climbed in the car, there was already 1 person in the car and one of the others climbed in after me, the other 2 got in the front, this was it wasn't it? I could already see the headlines tomorrow:

Lance Is Dead!

Chapter Sixteen

As I sat there in the car between these 2 unknown people I was worried, what was going on here? I've clearly stumbled upon something that someone doesn't want getting out, this obviously has something to do with Maurice but what? What was this millionaire chestnut seller involved in? the people in car didn't speak to each other just merely grunted. The windows of the car were blacked out so I couldn't even see where we were going, after a couple of minutes one of them nudged me and nodded towards the window which they wound down, we were driving past Nancy's place and she was outside waiting for me, they clearly knew what my reaction would be and put their hands over my mouth, they kept the window down and nodded again to two more people in balaclava's walking towards Nancy, I tried to struggle then I felt a sharp pain in the back of my head, a trickle of blood rolled down my neck and I slipped into unconsciousness.

As I pulled down the blinds and turned the sign to 'Closed' I couldn't help feeling a little bit excited, for the first time in a long time I really felt like I had a genuine connection with someone, I finished putting the last few cups in the dishwasher and looked at the time 18:35, perfect I had just enough time to freshen up before we we're meeting. I ran back out to the front and pulled the cups out of the dishwasher I put them on the side and decided I'd put them away tomorrow, I put on my coat, went outside and locked the door behind me, I felt nervous waiting for him, I waited a few minutes and looked down at my phone '19:08' strange, he's never late? I was looking up and down the street, still no sign of him, I was starting to feel nervous now, had I been stood up? A car slowly rolled past and I felt like I was being watched, I didn't like that at all, I decided I'd go back inside the shop and wait there. I pulled the keys out of my pocket and started to try unlock the door, I was feeling nervous and creeped out so I was rushing and it took me a couple of attempts to get the key in the lock, I was about to unlock the door when I felt like someone was behind me, daring not to look I rushed to get in, but it was too late someone's hand was around my mouth and then everything went black.

When I finally came round my vision was blurry, my head was throbbing, I went to put my hand where the pain was to feel the damage but I couldn't move my hand, I was very confused, I blinked a few times and things started to come into focus, where was I? I looked around and I didn't recognise anything, I'd never been here before, the walls were lined with metal shelving and in the far distance I could see a door, I had no clue where I was I couldn't even think of anywhere remotely similar, all I knew is I was definitely in trouble. It dawned on me my arms were tied behind the back of the chair I was sat on, the last thing I remember was being in the car and seeing Nancy, then I remembered the men approaching her, panic set in and I frantically tried to free my hands the more I struggled the tighter it felt, I wasn't getting anywhere at this rate, I needed to calm down, I closed my hands and tried some breathing exercises that I'd read about online somewhere, unexpectedly this helped, I needed to calm down and focus, I needed to try and figure out where I was and how I could get out of here.

I'd been sat there for what felt like an eternity when finally the door opened, it slid to the side and 2 large figures walked in with a 3rd figure in their arms, I couldn't make out what was going on as it was at the other side of the room I was in, they sat the 3rd figure down and left, I heard them lock the door after, the echo of the lock mechanism echoed through the room. I tried calling to the person but there was no response, I tried to edge my seat over but I wasn't making very much headway, thankfully my feet weren't tied so I could use my legs to drag myself across the room, I did try walking initially but I was still feeling a little light headed from the blow earlier in the car, it took me a few minutes to make it close to the person and then it dawned on me, the person slumped on the chair was Nancy, I frantically tried to wake her, thankfully I couldn't see any signs of injury but she was out for the count.

After 10 minutes or so eventually Nancy began to come around, I was so relieved she was ok but I couldn't help feeling guilty, this was all my fault after all, she looked up at me *'Lance? Where are we? Whats going on?'* I looked at her and replied *'Nancy, I'm so glad you're ok, I honestly don't know where we are, someone threw me in the back of a car and knocked me out, I woke up here a while ago and then they brought you in after, I'm sorry this is all my fault'* Nancy looked at me and smiled *'Lance, none of this is your fault, you didn't bring me here, you didn't attack me, do not blame yourself for this'* I couldn't help but feel touched by what she said, I was amazed at how incredible she was *'are you ok? what did they do to you are you hurt?'* *'Nothing I'm fine, they put something over my mouth and that's the last thing I remember'* I was concerned but she didn't appear to be hurt so hopefully that's all that happened, before I could say anything suddenly her expression changed *'Lance your tied up? Hold on let me try get you out'* in all honesty I'd completely forgotten about that as I was too concerned for Nancy, she got up and walked around the back and messed around with the ties for a minute or two and then managed to get my hands free I instinctively started rubbing my wrists, *'How did you manage that?'* I asked, she smiled and showed me her keys, one was jagged and she managed to cut through with that, I stood up and hugged her.

I spent the next 10 minutes explaining to Nancy, what had happened, I told her everything, the pictures, the meeting with Shane, the suspicions about Maurice and the people in the balaclava's, we sat for a moment in silence *'I'm sorry Nancy, I had no idea about any of this'* she put her hand on mine and said *'Lance, you haven't done anything, we don't even know what's going on, lets just focus on getting out of here'* she was right. I started looking around for a way out, a window, a vent, anything, but there was nothing, I climbed up on some of the shelves but there was no way out except the door we came in through and I already knew that was locked up good *'Lance quick, get back over here now!'* I went back over and she gestured to my chair, she sat back on hers and gestured *'shh'* then I realised someone was coming, I heard the lock on the door open and another person was laid in the room, this time they were unceremoniously just dropped in as the door closed I heard a man's deep voice *' I can't believe she scratched me, feisty one is that'* the door was locked again, they didn't even bother to check on me or Nancy, then something dawned on me *'She?'* I suddenly wished I was still unconscious.

Nancy rushed over to the body and called me over *'Lance she's still breathing but she's unconscious, isn't this your work friend?'* I walked over and Aimee was laid on the floor *'Yeah she is, what have they done to her?'* Nancy looked at me and I looked back at her, I'd omitted any details around Aimee and never mentioned pictures of the two of us *'Why would they have brought her too?'* I felt myself going red *'I'm not sure, maybe they've been following me for a while and saw us at the restaurant that night and got the wrong end of the stick?'* I walked over hoping Nancy bought my story, I really didn't want to go into any more detail, I looked Aimee over and I could see her lip was bleeding and her cheek was raised and red, she'd clearly put up a fight. It took a few minutes but eventually Aimee came round *'Lance? Whats going on? Who's this?'* I helped Aimee up and helped her into one of the chairs, I explained the situation again carefully omitting certain details, this was not an ideal situation and certainly not one I wanted to be caught in the middle of right now.

'So this is all something to do with the case you've been working? I still don't understand why we're here and the pictures you mentioned? Why are you being followed?' I looked at her for a moment and said *'I honestly wish I had answers for you, that's what I've been trying to find out, it looks like theres more to this than meets the eye and I've*

kind of got myself in abit of trouble and I'm sorry but I've got you tied up in it all too' she looked at me for a moment and then got up and started to pace the room we were in. I looked over at Nancy who looked less than impressed I walked over to her to ask if she was ok but before I opened my mouth she turned on her heel and also began pacing the room, I couldn't help but wish someone would come and drag me away, I immediately regretted feeling this way when I heard someone coming, I told the girls to get to the back of the room as the door opened, 3 large individuals, faces still covered beckoned me over, 3 against 1, I didn't stand much chance so I just co-operated they grabbed me and dragged me off, locking the door behind us.

We walked for a minute or two in silence anytime I tried to speak one of them just shook his head at me, they pushed me through a door a few corridors down and I was in an office, they sat me down in a chair and put a glass of water in front of me, there I took a drink and looked around to assess my surroundings, a relatively desolate office, a table, some chairs and then a CCTV set up in the corner, one of the screens showed the room I was previously in, my heart sank as I could clearly see Nancy and Aimee in deep conversation, for a moment I forgot where I was then one of the men put a phone down on the table and hit loud speaker.

'Lance, what exactly are you looking for?'

I didn't recognise the voice, although the quality of the call was poor so I doubt I'd even recognise it even if I did know who it was

'I'm sorry? Who am I speaking to?' I replied *'Lance, we both know I'm not going to tell you that, you need to listen to me and listen to me good, you have 2 choices, you either stop what you're doing or you're going to sit there and watch those 2 girls die on the screen in front of you'* I felt all the colour drain out of my face *'Look, I don't know whats going on, I was simply writing a peace on a man I'd spoken to every morning, I thought it was strange there was no investigation so I dug a little deeper, I didn't intend on stepping on any toes, I can end*

this now, let the girls go and its done, I'll stop, I don't even know what I'm looking for' my voice was shaking, I didn't care what happened to me at this point but I couldn't let anything happen to either of those two *'Ok Lance, you seem like a man of your word, we can end all of this now, but Lance, I'm also a man of my word, if you continue what you're doing you'll regret it'* I knew they were being serious and this was not someone I wanted to mess around with *'Ok then let them go, I want to see them get out of here unharmed, but I want you to know, I wasn't looking for anything or trying to out anyone, I just wanted to know what happened'* the voice let out a sinister sounding laugh *'Don't you worry about Maurice'* and then hung up, I was rocked to my core, I felt sick.

The men left me sat there for a minute or two and then grabbed under my arms and took me back to the room with the girls, part of me was hoping they'd let them go before letting me go, that was a whole other issue I was not looking forward to dealing with. As we got back to the room they opened the door, one of them went in and beckoned the girls forward, they stood us all in a line in front of them and pushed me in the back with what was quite clearly a gun, we started walking in silence, we walked down a few corridors, none of which were heading back towards the office, I glanced out of the windows and it hit me, I knew exactly where we were, we were at the warehouse Maurice and Shane had their run in, now I was really nervous, was this Shane's doing? We rounded a corner and one of the men put his hand on my shoulder to stop me, I looked at him and he pointed towards a door at the end of the corridor and pushed me forward, I guess this was the way out, we all walked towards the door and the men turned and went back the other way, even though I could tell she was still mad at me Nancy still gripped my arm tightly, we all walked towards to the door together, we were about 5 feet away when the door burst open and I was staring down the barrel of a gun.

'SHANE!?'

Chapter Seventeen

As I stood there staring down the barrel of Shane's gun, I felt Nancy's grip on my arm loosen and her pull away and Aimee took a step to the side, *'Shane?'* I asked again he looked at me puzzled *'Lance? What are you doing here?'* he lowered his gun, I couldn't help but be relieved, for a moment I thought this was all Shane's doing *'I don't think now is the time or place to discuss, what are you doing here?'* I asked *'Well, I was in the area and I drove past and saw some shifty looking people in balaclava's walking through the door, I think its best you come down to the station and we can talk about whats happening here'* I agreed, Shane looked at Aimee and Nancy *'I think you two need to come as well'* Nancy agreed but Aimee wasn't so cooperative, she refused and pushed her way past me and outside. Before anything else could happen I could hear running behind us and something that distinctly sounded like the cocking of a gun, without hesitation I grabbed Nancy, look at Shane and said *'Run'* as we set off the people who pointed us towards the door had returned, this time there was no friendly warning as they rounded the corner they each let off a few shots, we heard them hit the door behind us, a fraction slower and it would've been us they hit, Shane grabbed Aimee and we all ran to Shane's patrol car *'In now all of you'* we all jumped in Shane's car and we sped off, I looked back just in time to see them opening the door.

My heart was pounding, I leaned back in the front seat and closed my eyes, what is going on? I tried to fathom what I'd stumbled upon but nothing made sense, I opened my eyes and looked in the rear view mirror, Nancy was staring out of the window, Aimee, was not, Aimee was staring a hole straight through me. I realised I hadn't had chance to fill Aimee in or explain the situation *'So*

Aimee, There's something I need to tell you, I'm sorry you've been dragged into all this but well..' and before I could finish 'This better be good Lance' she interrupted sternly, I sheepishly explained the whole thing, start to finish, I told her about visiting the house, the library and the photo's, we all then sat there in silence whilst Aimee processed the whole thing. I gave it a few minutes then looked in the rear view mirror again, see if I could get a feel for the mood, this time both Aimee and Nancy were staring out of the windows, we were in for a long ride back to the station, so I decided to kill the time by telling Shane exactly what had gone down that day.

After what felt like an eternity, we finally arrived back at the station, Shane leaned into the back and asked the girls if they wanted to come in and discuss what was going on or did they want to go home, they both decided to stay, we all got out of the car and followed Shane into the precinct, he walked over to the front desk and made it clear he was not to be interrupted, he walked into his office and beckoned us in. We all took a seat in Shane's office, he'd already sent someone out to get coffee's and told us to prepare for a long stint, he told us to give him a few minutes to set everything up, I had no idea what he was doing or what exactly he was setting up, Nancy excused herself to the bathroom and I wanted to get up and stretch my legs but before I did Aimee stopped me 'Lance, who exactly is that girl and why is she here? Are you and her an item? I don't mind I'd just like to know' I was taken aback by her forwardness, however I knew what Aimee was like and I should've expected this 'Nancy is just a friend, we do spend time together but its not like we're sleeping together or anything' I responded, I mean, technically I wasn't lying, this seemed to be a good enough explanation for Aimee as she smiled and said 'Ah ok, I was just wondering that's all' and sat back in her chair, I couldn't help but feel like I'd dodged a bullet 'I suppose we all kiss friends so its not unusual I guess' she said without even looking in my direction, my heart sank, I didn't know how to respond and luckily I didn't have to, Nancy walked back in and Shane was all set up.

I looked around the room, it was various copies of all the newspaper articles I'd found and the pictures of us that came through my door along with a bunch of other stuff I hadn't seen before, Shane stood up *'Ok guys, so some of this you may have seen before, some you haven't, as I told Lance, I've been looking into this for a while, I couldn't link anything up and nothing seemed to make sense, then I was speaking to Lance about something that went down years ago at the warehouse you were at today and on the way back here I thought this was too much of a coincidence so I've decided 4 heads are better than 1, now this is entirely optional and you're free to leave at anytime, but I think all 4 of us together can figure out whats going on here because I think its clear this isn't just an ordinary case Lance has picked up'* I looked at him and told him I was in, Nancy agreed and after a few moments so did Aimee. We spent the next few hours combing over all the articles about Maurice's heroics and all the amazing things he did, Shane eventually called for us to take 5, the girls left the room and it was just me and Shane, I decided to ask about the house he took me *to 'Shane, there's something I still don't understand, Maurice's body was found in supposedly his penthouse yet you took me to a house? Am I missing something?'* he smiled at me and told me I was sharper than I looked he explained that both belonged to Maurice, his body was found in his penthouse however the body was in an unidentifiable condition, the body had been burned and technically it hadn't been confirmed whether it was actually Maurice and there was no evidence the incident *actually* happened in the building, there was nothing at all to suggest there was any sort of fire, no smoke damage and frankly everything was in perfect condition, coincidentally the two days leading up to the body being found and the day after the CCTV in the building had been cut off, the only reason this was noticed was when we asked to see the footage, noone appeared to even know it had been cut off as there was still a feed running but it appeared to be on a separate channel and was just dead footage that wasn't being saved anywhere, the house I visited with Shane was where Maurice spent most of his time.

I sat there for a moment trying to take everything in *'Didn't anyone question the staff?'* I asked *'We tried, but they all stuck to the same story, they didn't see anyone that night and there was no rota and apparently there was never a rota , we brought them all in for questioning but there wasn't anything we could do so we had to release them, we've tried to contact them since but they all gave false information and had false supporting documents so we have no trace'* he sat down on the corner of his desk and ran his hand through his hair in frustration, there was something missing and noone could put their fingers on it. Nancy walked back in the room a minute or two later on her own Shane asked where Aimee was and Nancy explained she was taking a call but would be back in soon, eventually Aimee came back and apologised for holding us up, we all went back to scouring the articles and we were at it for quite some time until Nancy broke the silence *'If Maurice was so good, why did he retire early? There's been no suggestion of injury or any kind of mentally scaring incident? And surely only having an officers salary and chestnut selling wouldn't make him a millionaire? Did he have another source of income?'* I looked up at Shane waiting for an answer, Shane looked thoughtful for a moment and then responded *'Maurice was prolific, he brought down a lot of high level criminals and even took down a whole syndicate, I always suspected he retired early through fear of retribution, he wasn't a millionaire when he left the force, I can assure you of that, I've looked through his file and it simply says 'retired' there's no elaboration'* I could tell Shane was fed up of hitting dead ends too *'I've also noticed something else, it seems that over the course of his career he was decorated and each time he received a commendation if you look closely at the pictures, who's this guy on the front row?'* Nancy said, Shane took the clippings Nancy was holding and examined them for a moment *'Now I cant be sure but it looks like an old officer who, well I shouldn't really be saying this so nothing said leaves this room, but well, he was caught taking handouts from criminals to overlook them, I guess he was bitter because Maurice ended up cleaning up his buddies'* We all sat back in our chairs, exhausted but determined.

I looked at my phone 04:58, the girls were asleep in their chairs and had been for a couple of hours, in fairness it had been a long day, kidnapped and locked in a room and now investigating a potential murder case, me and Shane kept at it, relentless, tirelessly pouring through pages and pages, then suddenly Shane sat bolt up right *'Lance, look at this'* I walked around to Shane's desk, he'd been looking at Maurice's personal file, it was a list of all Maurice's partners, there was only 1 after Shane a 'Richard 'Rich' Newhall' I looked at him and asked *'Is this name supposed to mean anything Shane?'* he looked at me and clicked Rich's name, it was the same guy who was in all the pictures, the one who had been taking handouts, Shane looked at me and said *'Lance, do you think Maurice knew? Do you think he was in on the handouts?'* I sat for a moment and thought about it *'Do you think Rich had something to do with Maurice's death? Do you think he was bitter all these years Maurice put all his friends behind bars and waited long enough for noone to make the connection? Wait.. What if Rich is the one pulling the strings? Maybe he's the one who's been getting people taking pictures, maybe once he left the force he joined his friends on the other side, do you think it was him on the other end of the phone?'* I think Shane could tell there was excitement in my voice *'Lets not get carried away here Lance, but I think we might be onto something'*

After that we decided to call it a night, Shane dropped us all off home and told me he'd be in touch, once I got home I was too excited to sleep, this was it, finally we were getting somewhere, I didn't care about my story anymore, this was something much bigger, truth be told, I probably wasn't even going to write an article on it, I got in to bed and my mind was buzzing, for the first time in a long time I went to sleep happy. I was awoken a few hours later by my phone ringing, I picked it up and looked *'Unknown Caller'* I looked at it for a moment and thought about ignoring it but I answered, and I wish I didn't *'tut tut Lance, I told you to leave well alone and you'd be fine, but here you are running off to Shane Hennessey, guess we'll be seeing you soon'* and hung up, I froze, it was the same person who I spoke to on the phone in the warehouse, how did they know? Not only what I was doing but who with? And how did they get my number, panic set in and I tried to call Shane, I couldn't get through it just rang out, I tried 2 or 3 times to no avail, this wasn't good, I quickly typed out a text *'We need to meet up, Now, get to Nancy's coffee shop'* and hit send, I sent it to both Aimee and Shane, I sent a separate message to Nancy asking her to close the shop and we'd be there as soon as we could.

20 minutes later I was outside Nancy's shop, I was nervous, I was panicking and I couldn't help but look over my shoulders every few seconds, who even knew if anyone else was going to turn up, I tried the door but it was locked, I knocked on the window and Nancy peered through one of the blinds, she unlocked the door, tears streaming down her face and threw her arms around me *'Lance, I got a call and I don't know what to do'* I felt the colour drain from my face, he had Nancy's information too? I hugged her tightly and told her everything was going to be ok, I explained that I'd asked Aimee and Shane to meet us there but I was struggling to get through to Shane, Aimee arrived around 15 minutes after me and she had also had a call, she was holding it together pretty well, she looked good too, she had her make up done and was wearing designer clothes, I couldn't help but admire her putting on a brave face. We all sat in relative silence cradling our coffee's, it was another hour before Shane arrived, when he got there he looked horrible, he seemed unnerved and couldn't relax, he looked at me and asked if anyone else had a strange call, Nancy was struggling to hold back tears hiding her face by taking a drink of her coffee, I explained we'd all had calls and it was the same voice from the warehouse, I took Shane to one side and I just asked outright *'Shane, was that Rich?'*

Shane looked at me as if he'd seen a ghost, he shook his head and looked me dead in the eye *'Lance, I don't know how to tell you this but.. that voice.. was Maurice'*

Chapter Eighteen

As we all sat there around the table in silence, I couldn't help but wonder exactly what was going on? Its not like I was trying to out someone or get someone in trouble, how did it come to this? All I was trying to do was get my big break and in the end all I've done is endangered people who I care about. The silence was finally broken by Shane *'Ok, we need to do something about this, we're all clearly in danger but at least we're in this together, I think the best course of action is so none of us get caught out alone, we stick together, Nancy how long can you close the shop for?'* Nancy thought for a moment *'I guess I can close it for as long as needed?'* Shane gave her a comforting smile *'Perfect, ok listen to me, I want everyone to go home, collect the essentials, things they might need for a few days camping out here, just whilst we get a plan together and I want everyone back here within the hour? Ok?'* everyone agreed.

Nancy already had everything she needed and Aimee headed out, I couldn't help but be most worried about her, she hadn't been the same since the kidnapping, she was being cold and distant towards me but in her defence, that was justified, I felt she was putting on a brave face as she wasn't upset or didn't seem affected but I could tell deep down she was worried, I walked out of the shop, buttoned up my coat and put on my gloves as I set off I couldn't help but feel nervous every footstep sounded louder and louder and I felt worried walking towards people, just as I was thinking I was being silly I felt a strong grab on my arm, panicked I spun round, closed my eyes and threw a punch, the hand didn't let go and pulled me down with it *'Well, at least you have a good punch on you Lance'* I opened my eyes to see Shane holding his jaw, he got up and helped me up *'Come on, lets walk and talk'*

We'd been walking for a little while and neither of us had said a word, I felt uneasy, we finally got to my apartment block and Shane ushered me inside, part of me was worried that this was all going to turn around and once we were inside Shane was going to get rid of me, I shook it off and thought to myself how silly I was being, we walked up the stairs and into my apartment, Shane walked in behind me and I heard him put the lock on, I spun round and he gestured for me to sit on the sofa, I sat down and he sat next to me *'Lance, I want to ask you something and I want you to be honest with me'* I nodded and agreed *'How well do you know Aimee? I mean.. Lance, I've been on the force for some time and people who have been kidnapped against their will aren't ok for a while, Aimee seems to have bounced straight back?'* I looked at him and thought for a moment *'I mean, I haven't known her for long but the time I have known her, she's a strong, independent woman she's fierce and unafraid of the world, she's smart and clever, I think this is a front and in reality she's scared, I think we'll see when we get back to the coffee shop the real Aimee'* he looked at me for a moment, picked up my phone and passed it to me *'Call her'* I looked at him puzzled but I unlocked my phone and hit call, *Nothing*, I tried again with the same result *'Maybe she's busy packing her stuff?'* Shane looked at me with a raised brow, smiled and shook his head.

An hour later we were back at the coffee shop, I was there, Shane was there and Nancy was there, *'Where's Aimee?'* asked Nancy innocently, I looked at Shane, he took a sip of coffee and exhaled *'Well, if I'm being honest, I don't think she's coming, I've been concerned ever since we we're back at the station, she didn't seem interested in helping us and whilst we we're here she didn't seem too concerned about her call, I don't think she's been entirely truthful with us, I think theres something about Aimee we don't know and that she isnt telling us, Lance?'* I sat there and thought for a moment, then I remembered something *'Well.. There was this one time, we were at her place and she took a phone call in the bathroom? I mean maybe it was a private call, I've never really thought about it?'* Shane looked at me *'What kind of situation was this? And how long had you known her? We're you having dinner? Were you picking something up?'* I looked sheepishly over at Nancy *'Well, we'd known each other a short while but I was..'* I stalled for a moment and thought about how I could say this next part *'I eer was staying the night'* Shane looked at me as did Nancy, neither looked phased, maybe I was arrogantly thinking Nancy would've been hurt by hearing that, I mean in reality we were nothing more than friends so why would she care? *'So Lance, let me get this right, a woman you had only known for a short while, you were spending the night and she left what I assume to be an intimate situation to take a call in the bathroom? Did that not seem off to you?'* I thought for a moment *'Well no? maybe it was a private call?'* I retorted *'Lance, if you barely knew her and she you, then even if it was a private call you wouldn't have known who she was speaking to even if she said a name right? Don't you think it's odd she was going out of the way to make sure she wasn't heard by you?'* I sat and thought for a moment *'I mean at the time no, wait, Shane, what are you saying?'* I could feel myself getting annoyed *'What I'm saying Lance is, by any chance did Aimee start showing an interest in you around the time you began looking into this with Maurice? Did things move quickly from acquaintance to something a little more? You're naïve if you cant connect the dots'* I sat down for a moment, how could I be so stupid?

We spent 3 days holed up in the coffee shop, stepping outside only briefly for some fresh air or a cigarette in Shane's case, always in a 2 and never for more than 5 minutes, we'd been pouring over all the information I had collated and Shane had made 1 trip back to the precinct to explain he would be working from out of his office for a few days and he brought back a few files, we were getting nowhere and there had been no more phone calls, noone heard from Aimee and I still couldn't get through to her, I'd tried calling and I'd even sent her a message asking if she was ok, nothing, I was really hoping Shane had got it all wrong about her. If I was being honest with myself I was starting to go a little crazy being all cooped up, Nancy was having a nap in the store room out back, we'd set up a couple of tents and sleeping bags and kept the blinds down at all times, I called Shane over who looked deep in thought *'Shane, Why don't we go back to wherever you took me claiming to be Maurices place? See if we can find something?'* he looked at me and said *'Claiming? Lance that was Maurice's place, the Penthouse was just his city home, he was barely there, which is even more suspicious that's where the body was found, there's no way we could go the penthouse, we could go back to the house but I don't know what we'll find, what exactly are you thinking of?'* truth be told I wasn't sure myself *'Well, we never got upstairs and I mean most places that big have an office of sorts? Maybe theres something we can find and we'll see exactly whats going on? Maybe a ledger? Receipts?'* Shane smiled for the first time in days *'Receipts?'* he let out a little laugh and I guess I saw the funny side too I couldn't help but smile but it was nice to smile again, *'Ok Lance, screw it, we haven't got anything else, there's one condition, Nancy doesn't find out'* I agreed.

Obviously I was keen to get things moving and I said we should go tonight, we haven't heard anything in a while and on top of that surely whoever made those calls, I know Shane suspected it was Maurice but I wasn't convinced, surprisingly Shane agreed, I guess he was starting to feel a little caged in too *'What exactly do you plan to do about Nancy by the way?'* I asked *'Don't you worry about that Lance'* he said with a smile. I looked down at my phone, 10:02 *'Right come on you two, I've had enough of been cooped up for a few hours time for a change of scenery'* said Shane out of nowhere, he threw me his keys and told me to get in the car, I did as he said and went and sat in the car, Shane had already told me earlier, he intended on taking Nancy to his office and have her stay there and look through old files and he was going to tell her he was taking me to stake somewhere out, actual police work, I hoped she'd buy this. 20 minutes later we were at the precinct, Shane walked up to the desk and told the officer behind that Nancy would be in his office working and he did not want her to be disturbed, strangely the officer never questioned this but I put it down to the respect Shane commanded, we left Nancy to it and he handed me a bullet proof vest and we headed back to the car.

We set off back to Maurice's house and we were casually chatting probably for the first time since I'd ever met Shane, he told me about back in his younger days he was quite the amateur boxer but decided his dreams lay in the force rather than in the ring and I told him about why I moved out to the city he told me he respected me for at least having the balls to leave everything behind and chase my dream, I couldn't help but feel like I was starting to warm to Shane. Eventually we arrive back at the house, this time we drove a block away and decided to head there on foot so we could be more stealthy, Shane told me to take off my vest, I was apprehensive but he told me we might aswell walk in wearing neon clothes if we we're sneaking around with the word 'Police' in bright yellow emblazoned across our chests, I guess I understood his logic and I took it off, at least this time I knew what I was getting myself into so I was more prepared than last time, we waded through some bushes and climbed over a low wall heading into the back yard, we snuck across to a back door and thankfully it was unlocked.

As we crept in I couldn't help but feel like I was a teenager again sneaking into abandoned buildings, I smiled to myself and carried on, we headed straight for the spot we hid away in last time, we'd already agreed we want to stop here first and then assess whether we were alone or not, we waited for a minute or two and heard nothing, it seemed the coast was clear. We carefully entered each room making sure to avoid windows or any area's lit by street lights or moonlight, we each had a small torch that wouldn't be easy to spot, we rummaged through drawers and books on the shelves, all I came across we're novels and standard books, honestly I was a little disappointed, it seemed an old library had a clear out and Maurice just took the lot, most of the books looked untouched, I suppose I didn't really know what to think and then I heard Shane shouting *'Lance, upstairs'* I put the book back and like an excited kid I headed towards the stairs.

We left the spot we we're hiding in last time, I felt uneasy as I watched him head straight off to the rooms we went into last time, I didn't like what was going on but I didn't have much choice now did I? I nonchalantly wandered around the hall way looking at the paintings and the dust gathered on their frames, such a waste, although I may not look the type, I did enjoy the arts, I gave it a few minutes and took a deep breath, I suppose its time to start making a move. I headed up stairs avoiding the first room with the light on, I headed to one of the rooms further away, I walked over to the window, a familiar view, one I had grown to like, it looked out across some nice gardens and in the distance you could make out the skyline of the city, I smiled and headed out of the room, I guess it was now or never, I headed towards the room with the light and entered closing the door behind me. Everything was exactly as I had left it, a small lamp was lit in the corner just bright enough to dimly light the room, the blinds drawn, a small book I had found in one of the desk drawers and ah yes, an unconscious Aimee handcuffed to the chair *'Lance, upstairs'* I called, I heard him rushing up the stairs and he burst in through the door, a look of horror on his face *'Shane? What have you done?'*

Chapter Nineteen

As I stood there completely dumbfounded at the scene in front of me, I repeated myself, 'Shane? What have you done?' I could feel the anger building up inside me, I could feel my fists clench into a ball at my side, as I started to walk towards them, Shane turned around and looked out of the window behind them, peering through the closed blinds, I knelt down next to Aimee and put my hand on her face, she was still alive at least, I couldn't see or feel any blood so I was at least sure he hadn't hurt her. Shane walked past me and perched himself on the edge of a desk 'Lance, do you not find it odd?' I turned to him, confused and replied 'What?' he looked for a moment and then continued 'Lance, it's her, Aimee, she clearly has something to do with all this, I touched upon it before but you showed the same level of ignorance and blind faith in your, hmm, acquaintances? Shall we say? You choose to believe everything they say without question, Why wasn't she worried about receiving a mysterious call from someone she didn't know? Why was there no real fear in her when she was kidnapped for absolutely no reason then imprisoned and subsequently let leave with no explanations whatsoever? Are you really that naïve?' I looked at him and for a moment, he was right.

I walked over to the window Shane had looked out of before and took a look out myself, I couldn't help but think he was making a lot of sense, I mean why would someone as intelligent and well linked as Aimee be interested in someone like me? I'd kind of thought about this before but I just put it down to opposites attract, but now I can't help but wonder, all the things she did for me, the meetings with Quentin, getting me invited to the ball, was Shane right after all? I turned to Shane 'Do you have any proof? Or is this just assuming?' he threw me Aimee's phone 'Lance, there's nothing in the call logs to say she even got a call' I didn't want to believe what he was saying 'How did you even unlock it?' he smiled at me and said 'An unconscious person is hardly going to put up a fight to give me their thumb print now are they?' he was right, I felt pretty ridiculous after asking. I stood for a few minutes scrolling through the call log unable to see anything that suggests Aimee had the same call as the 3 of us, I decided to scroll through her messages to see if I could find anything else, I knew I shouldn't but I was trying to clear her name after all, I opened up her chat logs but all that was there was 'Quentin' and 'Lance' 'I mean I know there's no proof she had a call but there isn't anything to say she hasn't either, maybe she deleted it, could you blame her? Maybe she thought if she ignored it then it would go away?' I knew as soon as I said it I sounded ridiculous 'There you go again, always trying to see the good in people, Sometimes it just isn't there'

'What exactly do you plan on doing with her?' I asked 'I just want to ask her some questions, she should be coming round pretty soon' I didn't like where this was going but at the same time I didn't want to be here when she woke up either, I didn't want her to think I was in on this 'Shane, I don't want to be around when she wakes up, this was nothing to do with me' Shane looked over to me 'Exactly as I expected, you don't have to be here, just make sure you're in ear shot, I want you to hear it with your own ears exactly what she has to say' I nodded, I could see where he was coming from and he was right I feel I at least deserve some answers if Aimee really is in on this. I decided to leave the room, there was another small table off to the side of the door holding an empty vase, I moved the vase onto the floor and perched myself on the desk, hoping it was strong enough to hold me, I took out my phone and decided to message Nancy to make sure she was ok.
As I watched him leave the room and close the door behind him, leaving it open slightly just enough for it not to be noticed, I grabbed a bottle of water I'd left on the side and splashed it in Aimee's face, needless to say this roused her, she sat for a moment

blinking rapidly and blowing the water out of her mouth, she tried to move her hands and then realised she couldn't, her eyes darted around the room until they landed on me in the corner. Once her eyes had focused and Aimee realised who I was, she gave me a scowl 'Shane, what is going on?' I walked over to her and sat back on the edge of the desk 'I know everything Aimee, I want you to come clean, I want you to tell me everything' she looked up at me 'What are you talking about? Let me go, this isn't funny Shane' I looked at her and our eyes met, she was angry, I could see the contempt she had for me burning in her eyes, I cupped her chin with my finger and thumb 'Aimee, people's lives are at stake, I don't know what you gain out of this and I certainly don't know what is going on, but it's obvious you're in on this with Maurice, I want you to tell me everything, you come clean here and now with me and when this is dealt with in the appropriate manner, I'll make sure you have no ties to any of this whatsoever' She pulled her face away from my hand, she scowled at me and said 'You're being ridiculous, I have no idea what's going on at all! I didn't know about any of this yet I was the one who ended up being kidnapped, twice!' tears started to roll down her cheeks but I wasn't buying it.

As I sat out on the hallway and listened to the back and forth between Shane and Aimee, I couldn't help but feel she was being honest and really had no idea what was going on but then again, this is exactly the point Shane was making, I was too quick to take everything on face value, I hated being here, I hated being a part of what was going on, I mean after all, technically I am an accomplice in all of this, unwittingly but still I am. I tried to listen in without being biased to believe everything Aimee was saying, however I did feel it was suspicious all her chat logs had either been deleted or she only spoke to me and Quentin, I knew she was career driven but I don't believe her life revolved around work that much. Although, my mind started to wander, perhaps not the best time, but it did, maybe she really was that career driven, I mean, she was close to Quentin and I made it clear my intention was to replace Quentin eventually, maybe she just wanted to cement her own future? Maybe I was over thinking things again but in the time I've known Aimee she's been nothing but honest and upfront with me, I always felt I was a good judge of character well, until I met Shane anyway, I still have no idea what's going on with him.

I stood up, I walked behind Aimee and paced back and forth 'Aimee, Look, I've been on the force for many years, I've got a lot of experience in dealing with these types of situations, maybe you've got yourself in trouble with the wrong people, maybe you've been working alongside them for a while and Lance just so happened to cross their paths in some coincidental way, regardless I don't believe you, I believe you have something to do with this, how else would they have direct contact with myself, Lance and Nancy? You never seemed afraid or like you were worried about your life or even showed any genuine concern for your safety, you barely spoke in the patrol car on the way back from the warehouse, you never really seemed or acted fazed back at the coffee shop where others were genuinely fearful and visibly shaken, you're hiding something and I want to know what it is and why' I circled back round and I was back in front of her, Aimee was scowling at me, the tears were now angry tears, just what I wanted, she was definitely about to slip up now. I didn't take my eyes off her until she started to talk, I felt I had a knack for reading people in these situations 'Did it ever occur to you Shane, that maybe it was me who was unfortunate enough to end up in all of this in a coincidental way? Maybe they had direct contact with you because Nancy owns a popular coffee shop, You are a renowned officer and Lance has hardly been the most stealthy person in the world trying to get information has he! You are all incredibly easily accessible, I have absolutely nothing to do with any of this, all I did was meet someone, we went out had a few good times and shared some interests, it was nice to finally have someone else, I've always been so wrapped up in my work I've never had the opportunity to just go out and have a good time, people at work don't want to hang out with the editor in chief's assistant because they think I'd tell their boss how they act outside of work, Lance was different, he was a nice, friendly guy he didn't try use me for my contacts or to further himself, and that's why I helped him, and what did I get for it? Strapped to a chair, twice! Shane I had nothing to do with this, I don't know what you think but you're wrong, just because you couldn't tell I was afraid or scared doesn't mean I wasn't, maybe your instincts aren't what they used to be! Now let me go!' I looked for a moment and for the first time, I wasn't 100% sure, I grabbed her phone and held it up and slide it back across the table towards her 'Then why is there no evidence of any calls from Maurice on your phone? You said you'd got the call didn't you?' she looked up at me with an angry scowl 'Are you actually that stupid? I walk around in the best designer clothes, the nicest shoes and expensive jewellery, does that phone look like its mine or does that look like a work phone?' I hadn't even thought about that, had I made a mistake?

The argument inside the room was getting more and more heated and I couldn't help but feel more and more awkward, I didn't want to be here in the first place, now I definitely didn't, Nancy wasn't answering my message but then again who could blame her for not responding, I selfishly couldn't help but think about myself, despite what was going on 10 feet away from me behind a door, I felt like I'd betrayed both Nancy and Aimee, I couldn't help but feel I wasn't at fault because it's not like anyone had ever said anything about being more than what we were but that was just me trying to justify everything. I couldn't take being sat there in silence any longer, I decided I needed a drink, I headed down stairs to the kitchen to get a glass of water, as I got to the bottom of the stairs I thought I could hear voices, but it wasn't Aimee or Shane's, it was multiple male voices, my eyes widened as I realised we were no longer alone. I put my hand over to my mouth to cover my heavy breathing, I panicked, I turned and tried to silently run back upstairs, I opened the door and saw Aimee sat there in tears her face flashed towards me and I saw the hurt in her eyes as she realised I was there the whole time. I ran over to them 'We're not alone, someone's here, we need to leave, now!' Shane's face drained of colour, without a word he turned to Aimee, uncuffed her and told us both to leave, Aimee grabbed her belongings and walked to my side 'Shane? Why aren't you coming?' he grabbed my hand, passed me his patrol car keys and said 'I'll tell you later Lance, get out of here, take Aimee with you, don't pick up Nancy, I want you to go straight to your apartment, I mean it Lance, both of you, straight there nowhere else, it's safer if Nancy doesn't know about any of this, don't worry about me I'll meet up with you later, get out of here, Now!' I didn't need telling again, I grabbed Aimee's hand, put my finger over my mouth and beckoned her. We crept down the stairs as quietly as we could, I could hear the voices in the room with the chestnut cart, I pulled Aimee to the spot me and Shane hid in the first time around, the coast was clear, we slipped out of the back door and ran to the edge of the garden. I glanced up and saw Shane peering out through the blinds, I hoped he knew what he was doing, I turned back around and led Aimee back to the patrol car, we climbed in and as I turned to Aimee, before I could say a word I was met with a hard slap across the face, well deserved I suppose.

'I deserved that' I said without breaking eye contact, I looked at Aimee in floods of tears and I grabbed her hand 'Aimee, you have to believe me, I had nothing to do with any of that, I had no idea what was going on and I certainly didn't know what Shane had done' she pulled her hand away from me 'Lance, I know you'd never do anything like that but where were you? You were obviously in that place, at some point you found out I was there and you knew what the situation was, why didn't you help me? Why did you let that happen?' I started the car and began to drive back to my place, I didn't respond straight away because honestly, I don't know why I let it happen either. I decided for the first time in a while I needed to be 100% honest with Aimee Look, I didn't know you were there until Shane took me to the house and shouted me upstairs, I was angry with him, he was saying you were involved and you and Maurice were in on this together, I refused to believe him, I told him you wouldn't do that but I let him convince me he would prove me right or wrong if I let him, I told him I wanted no part of this and I wanted him to let you go, he told me he would after he'd spoken to you, I refused to be in the room and I went outside and listened in, I knew you were innocent, but I wanted him to know it too' we sat there in silence for the rest of the drive. I knew Aimee was thinking things over and I wouldn't blame her if she wanted nothing to do with me ever again after this, the thought of that filled me with regret, I didn't want Aimee to not be around after this, all I could do was respect her wishes though and I'd said what I needed to say. Finally after what felt like an age, we arrived back at my apartment block, I parked the car a little away from the street as I didn't want it left out in the open and we got out, Aimee linked my arm and I couldn't help but feel a huge relief wash over me 'Look Lance, I know how things must have looked, I just wish you'd have stuck up for me, part of me feels like you didn't trust me after what you said in the car, you never asked me how I was, you asked Nancy but I didn't get any texts asking if I was ok or anything like that, I'm stubborn and I didn't feel good after finding out you and Nancy kind of had a thing going on and I was hurt when I realised you hadn't been honest with me about her, I just didn't want you to see it' I suddenly realised how awful I'd been, I just assumed because Aimee was such a strong person I didn't need to take care of her, I guess you never know what someone's going through or how they're feeling if you don't ask. I apologised to Aimee and I promised I'd never just assume things again, we headed to my apartment and we made small talk as we headed up the stairs, I unlocked the door to my apartment and we went inside, I turned on the lights and locked the doors behind us.

'Well, look who finally showed up'

I turned around and froze on the spot 'Maurice!?'

Chapter Twenty

I stood there, frozen, I couldn't believe what I was seeing 'Maurice? What is going on?' Maurice smiled at me and beckoned me to sit down on the sofa, somehow, I didn't feel like I had the option to refuse, I took Aimee's hand and we sat on the sofa together, I didn't like where this was going. 'Lance, you've been quite a busy bee lately haven't you? Running around town trying to dig up information on me, now listen, I'll tell you everything you want to hear, don't worry about that but not here, I have some associates on the way to pick us up to escort us to a more.. Familiar destination for us ok?' I sat there in silence, I didn't know what to think, I know I'd heard his voice but it still didn't seem real that he was alive, I thought maybe we were dealing with identity theft, I don't know I guess I was clutching at straws. We'd been sat for around 10 minutes when Maurice's phone buzzed, he looked over at us and smiled 'Please excuse me a moment' and headed off into my bedroom 'I don't like this Lance' whispered Aimee, truth be told, neither did I, Maurice still looked like a generally nice old guy, this entire scenario was bizarre, after a minute or two he emerged back into the living room 'Well, our ride is here, let's go' and he gestured towards the door, whilst there was nothing forceful or aggressive about the situation and the fact he appeared to be alone I certainly felt an aura about him that suggested the best thing was to do as he said, we made our way outside and we were greeted by a blacked out car 'Ok, let's go' said Maurice as he opened the back doors, we climbed in.

As we sat there in the back of the car, I was scared, I didn't want to show Aimee I was but deep down I was petrified, I couldn't help but fear for both our lives, Maurice had got into the passenger seat and was in conversation with the driver however we couldn't hear what they were talking about. I decided the best course of action for now was just to comfort Aimee, I put my arm around her and told her everything would be ok, she nodded and put her head on my shoulder, I looked around the car to see if there was a way out, not that I was expecting to find anything but I suddenly became aware of another car, exactly the same as this one, following behind us, obviously Maurice wouldn't be alone. We weren't in the car for very long, however I knew exactly where we were when we pulled up, despite it being dark I knew we were back at the warehouse, my heart sank a little, I was absolutely over seeing this place, nothing good ever happened here, the other car pulled up behind us, Maurice and the driver got out and the back doors were opened and we were gestured out, once we were out of the car we were flanked by 4 individuals, there was nowhere to go and no chance of escape.

We followed Maurice in total silence, we walked in through the door and we followed the corridors back around to the office I first spoke to Maurice after we'd been brought here the first time, he unlocked the door and in we went, two people followed us in and told us to take a seat and then left. Maurice paced the office for a minute and didn't say a word, he turned to me and smiled 'Lance, I know you'll have questions, but so do I, so let's make a deal, you answer my questions and we'll see if I answer yours after ok?' It didn't sound like I had much choice 'Maurice, before we do this, Aimee has nothing to do with any of this, Can't you let her leave? It's me you have a problem with so can't we deal with this just you and me?' I felt Aimee's grip tighten on my arm 'Sadly not Lance, she may alert someone to what is going on here, let's just see how this pans out ok? Now first of all I want to know exactly what you're doing, Why are you asking around after me and what are you trying to get out of this? As far as I can tell you're no police officer, no investigator, all you are is a journalist and from your work, not one that is very well thought of, now if you don't mind, I'd like to hear your answers as I'm starting to lose patience with you' his voice was angry, his words sinister but he still had a gentle smile on his face, this was not a good situation to be a part of.

'Ok, well, I'll be honest with you..' I told Maurice everything, I explained that I used to see him every day selling his chestnuts and we even occasionally exchanged pleasantries then one day when I went to pick up a story I saw his face and the headline, I told him I was in shock at what I'd seen and that I wanted to pick up the story, I explained everything I had done and the fact this was a genuine misunderstanding. So far he wasn't buying any of what I was saying, I could tell 'Carry on.. You haven't told me anything about why you've been trying to dig up any information on me yet' I could see he was getting impatient, I explained how all I was trying to do was get out of taking all the terrible stories no one else wanted and how I was just trying to further my career, I went on to talk about how I had no idea about anything until the night in the library when I was attacked. Maurice had stopped pacing around the room now and had taken a seat opposite us, I continued with what I was saying, I was trying to write a complementary piece on your life but then things turned sour for no reason, I had no idea about any of this and then I told him about Shane, I explained how Shane took me to his house and told me about his past, Maurice smiled' Ah yes, Shane, he always did talk too much, I'll have to discuss that with him next time we speak' I stopped talking and looked at Maurice 'Wait? Is Shane in on this? Does he have something to do with everything that's going on here?' Maurice silenced me with a look 'I told you I wanted my questions answering first, Continue' I suppose I didn't have any choice, I explained everything else that had happened, I explained about the trips to the house, the kidnappings, the phone calls, as I was telling Maurice everything that happened, I couldn't help but feel the anger inside me building up against Shane, this whole time, this whole damned time. Once I'd finished I looked at Maurice and said 'Look, you're either going to believe me or you're not, I had no idea about any of this, all I wanted was 1 good story, if you're going to kill me at least let Aimee go and answer my questions before you do'

Maurice looked at me and smiled 'Ok Lance, I'll tell you what, I'll answer your questions, what are they?' now that I was on the spot I was kind of unsure, I mean what did I want to know? What could I gain from this? Closure? I guess that was all really 'Right, well I want to know about Shane, Is he in on this or what? And I also want to know what's going on? How has all this happened? I don't understand how you went from being a revered police officer to a chestnut seller to whatever this is? Maurice, I don't know what I've stumbled upon but I'm just a regular guy, I saw someone I'd briefly met was dead and I thought I could use this to get my big break, I've clearly made a mistake and it looks like I'm going to pay for it, potentially with my life, the least you can do is tie up the loose ends for me?' he looked at me and smiled again, I didn't like it when he smiled, it's happened 3 times now and every time he does, he follows it with bad news 'Pay for it with your life?' he laughed 'Lance do I look like a killer to you?' I mean I guess he didn't but he also didn't look dead either so I didn't really know what I believed anymore.

'Fine, Fine, I'll tell you, I suppose Shane never told you why I left the force? If I was as revered as you believe I was? Well Lance, here's the scoop, I was a good cop, honestly I was the best, arrogant but true, I was an honest man getting by on a modest salary, I could live my life and I was relatively comfortable, I'd never been exposed to any corruption or any wrong doing, then one day I'm out on the beat and I caught a guy dealing, so I did the usual, I pinned him up, gave him the speech and cuffed him, I didn't have the patrol car so I radioed in for one and was told I'd have to wait, but I didn't mind, after all it was the right thing to do, so whilst we're sat there this guy starts talking about how he ended up dealing, the usual, bad childhood, bad neighbourhood. I told him none of that made him a bad person, but dealing did, and then he said something, he told me it didn't make him bad but it made him smart, he watched people struggle working and barely getting by and he looked at me and said just like you, but not me he said, I work when I want, I make as much as I want and then I do whatever I want, I looked at him and said but now you're caught and you can't, he laughed and said don't you worry about me, I'll be in the system for what? 6 months? I've never been caught before, then I'll go right back to it, rinse and repeat, I'm a winner. I looked him up and down and called him a punk, he told me maybe he was a punk but what did that make me when he was living the high life and I barely have a life, and it hit me, he was right, he knew he'd got to me and he looked me dead in the eye, straight faced and told me he could change my life, if I wanted what he had I could, I refused, I told him I was a man of the law and that's how I wanted to stay. He went silent for a minute and then asked me why that had to change, I told him a police officer doesn't sell drugs on the side, he told me I didn't have to, he gave me a proposition, he told me if I let him go today he'd give me a cut and then he'd carry on giving me a cut every month if I looked the other way, I told him no, he said look what do you have to lose? You walk away from here right now and you'll have a crisp $500 in your pocket, no one would know, you come back 1st of every month and you'll have the same again, maybe more. I told him to shut up, I sat there for another 10 minutes in silence, still waiting for this car to show up to book this guy, he was offering me what I would make in a week, and then he asked me, what do you have to lose? You accept and you get paid, I cross you and you know where I am you can arrest me again and throw away the key, I knew he was right, he told me to reach into his top pocket, I pulled out a wedge of cash Lance, more than I'd seen in a long time, I wanted it, he looked me in the eyes and said I know you want to take it all, but why take it all now and never get it again when you can take a cut and continue to get a cut for as long as you want, I knew it was wrong, I counted the cash, I took $500 put the rest back in his pocket and uncuffed him, I told him I'd be back on the 1st and he told me I wouldn't regret it, Lance I never did, that squad car didn't show up for another hour, all I had to do was tell them his gang friends showed up and I was outnumbered so I let him go, they bought it and I never looked back'

I sat there and took it all in 'But that doesn't explain how we've come to this here and now?' he looked at me and said 'Lance, do you think that was enough for me? Eventually I got greedy, I wanted more, so I started doing the same thing in a few more neighbourhoods, and when someone didn't pay, I made them, I became twisted, I lost my sense of justice because where was the justice? Why am I scraping by, risking my life every day and barely making it? These guys had it right, but I knew I had it better, I reaped all the rewards with none of the risk, within 2 years I had a racket going with my partner, I'm not going to discuss names but I was getting paid and that's all I cared about. Eventually people started catching on, it took around 5 maybe 6 years before I was called in to the superintendent's office, he told me there were suspicions but no proof, I denied everything and used my previous achievements as a solid back story, he agreed there would be no repercussions if I quit the force there and then, I strongly denied any wrong doing of any sorts and told him this was an injustice caused by my peers jealousy, however solely to uphold my reputation I would agree on the condition of a substantial payment he initially declined but I promised to go through the courts to fight this, I knew I wouldn't win but I also knew he didn't want all that hassle, we agreed somewhere in the middle of my request. I never stopped taking the cash from my rackets and now that I was able to dedicate all my time to it, I brought them all together into a syndicate, in the end, they did all the work and all I did was sit at the top, that's how we ended up here Lance, did you ever try buy and chestnuts from me? No and neither did anyone else, which is a good job, because in reality there were no chestnuts, the cart was a cover, sometimes it was drugs, sometimes it was money, but it was never chestnuts, I suppose I enjoyed the risk of being out in the open'

I sat there reeling from what I'd just heard, from a respected police officer to a chance meeting with a scum bag Maurice's entire life and values changed in an instant, Aimee hadn't said a word, she'd sat there with her head on my shoulder the entire time staring off into the distance, I didn't know what to say, I guess the only thing left to ask was 'What about Shane? How does he fall into all of this?' Maurice looked at me 'You really are convinced Shane is in on this aren't you?' I looked over 'I don't know, I can't decide, one minute I believe him and that he's helping me and the next he does something which completely throws me off, I just want the truth' Maurice cleared his throat 'Well, I'm sure he'll be arriving soon so why don't you ask him yourself?' and just as he finished his sentence Shane walked through the door with a smirk on his face 'Shane, your timing is impeccable'. He walked right up to Maurice and embraced him like an old friend, I couldn't believe what I was seeing, I was enraged 'Shane! How could you? How could you do this to me? To us?' Shane looked right through me and didn't say a word, Maurice put his hand on Shane's shoulder 'Shane, take care of our little problem please' Did he mean us? 'Wait..!' before I could even finish what I was about to say Shane pulled out a gun and fired, the echo of the shot ringing in my ears, all I could hear was Aimee screaming, How could he shoot her? She had nothing to do with any of this, this was all my fault, I tried to move but couldn't, then I realised, Shane hadn't shot Aimee, he'd shot me. Everything around me sounded muffled, like I was underwater, I heard another shot and that was it, Shane had done it, Me and Aimee, I slumped down out of my seat and the room was fading, I faintly heard the door bang open and footsteps followed, everything went black, then nothing.

Chapter Twenty One

All I could see was a blinding bright white light, I had always been a sceptic and thought once you were gone, you were gone, no light, no seeing the people you've lost just nothingness, it was a strange feeling washing over me, I didn't feel any pain, so at least it must have been quick, I tried to walk towards the light as I assumed that's what I was supposed to do, but I couldn't move, my legs wouldn't work, I tried to lift my hand to shade my eyes from the harsh light but they wouldn't move either. I was just there, alone wondering why I couldn't move, then the light momentarily disappeared like an eclipse from the brightest light to pitch black, then it was back again, the darkness came and went in a moment, was this me slipping away? Why was it taking so long? I was sure I could hear something in the distant, something that sounded like a very soft sobbing, I could feel a warmth on the side of my face I tried to ignore it and was trying to listen for the sound again to see if I could decipher where it was coming from, ever so slightly the sound got louder, as if it was coming towards me, I was struggling to grasp what was going on, then it happened again, just like before a darkness consumed the light momentarily and then drifted back away, what was going on? The sound I could hear was getting louder, closer and more frequent, I still had no power over my body so I couldn't seek it out, I could feel my chest getting tighter and my head began to pound, my lungs exploded with the deepest of breaths and my eyes sprung open, I heard someone shout 'He's awake!' my eyes burned so intensely I could hardly stand to keep them open, I squinted to try and make them adjust to my surroundings, it took a few seconds but eventually they focused, I was staring up at a bright white light. I turned my head to the side to get away from the light, all I could see was medical equipment, and all I could feel was a searing pain down my left side, I tried to sit up but couldn't move, it was agonising to try, the door opened and in walked a nurse 'Good to see you've finally come round Mr Malone, looks like the surgery was a success' she smiled and took my temperature, surgery? What? I tried to ask but before I could say a word she said 'Maybe rest before trying anything, I'm sure you'll be brought up to speed in no time' with that she smiled again and left, dimming the lights as she did, I had no idea what was going on, I closed my eyes and drifted off into an uneasy sleep.

I woke up a few hours later, still laying in the hospital bed, I had no idea what had happened or how I got here, the last thing I remember was Shane and Maurice embracing like old friends then Shane turning his gun on me, I thought I was dead, well who's to say I'm not, maybe this is me in limbo, maybe I'm just waiting for the end, I laid there for a moment contemplating my life. I was brought back to earth when the door opened to my room 'Lance, you're awake' it was Aimee, I looked at her confused 'Aimee? What's going on?' she came and sat by my bedside and took my hand 'We thought we'd lost you' tears rolling down her cheeks 'We?' I was well and truly confused now, I had no idea what was going on and Aimee didn't seem in a rush to tell me, 'Aimee please tell me what happened back there?' she wiped her tears and smiled, 'I'm not sure how to explain anything that happened, can this wait? I don't think I'm the right person to explain' I couldn't help but think if Aimee wasn't the right person then who was? I was too weak to keep asking, I gave up 'Ok, another time' we just stayed as we were for a while, no talking, no nothing, I kept drifting in and out of sleep but Aimee didn't leave my side.

It had been 3 days since I woke up in the hospital, Aimee had been in and out and Nancy had been to visit as well, I still had no idea what had gone on and anytime I mentioned it all I got was 'In due time' I was able to sit up now and was starting to get some movement back, it appeared Shane had missed his shot and got me right on the inside of my shoulder, I guess at least I was thankful to that. As I sat there I began to think about my life and the decisions I'd made, the more I thought about it the more I could see where Maurice was coming from, I've worked hard for so long and given it my all and what do I have to show for it? A tiny apartment on the outskirts of the city? Maybe I was over big city life, maybe it was time to give up on any ideas of being anything more than a small fry journalist. My thoughts were interrupted by the nurse coming in to check on me, she took my temperature and cleaned the wound, replacing the dressings and making sure everything looked alright, we indulged in small talk and she informed me I had a visitor, truth be told, I was happy for some company, she finished up and told me she'd send them in, I wondered whether it would be Aimee or Nancy, it was neither, the door opened and there stood a familiar figure 'Shane!?'

Shane walked into the room and sat beside me, he didn't say anything for a minute, was he here to finish the job? He looked at me and said 'Now, I know you have questions, Aimee told me you want to know what happened, right?' Aimee told him this? Was she in on this all along too? I could feel the colour draining from my face, the sudden realisation had I been played for a fool this entire time? 'Aimee? No?' he looked at me and smiled 'Lance, stop jumping to conclusions and listen to me, you want to know what happened don't you? Or have I wasted my time coming here?' I looked at him and I thought to myself if he really was here to finish the job surely it would've been done by now? 'Ok Shane, yes I'd like to know' he took a deep breath and sat back in the chair 'I thought so, Now, Before you and I met, I had my suspicions regarding Maurice in what little spare time I had I'd been trying to piece things together, but in reality, I had nothing, after Maurice's leaving celebrations I'd made the extra effort to stay in touch, I didn't tell you any of this before because I couldn't risk being compromised, it took a while but eventually Maurice brought me 'in' I'd built up trust and he thought I could be useful to him. I know what you're thinking, No I never did anything, I was never involved with any of his plans or schemes, I was just his man on the inside, all I had to do was make sure his dealings went uninterrupted, the problem was, he was careful, he never did anything himself, hell I had no idea about this whole Chestnut thing you knew about, I was starting to lose hope and thought I'd got myself in a bad situation and then you walked into my office, at first I didn't think anything of it, I tried to scare you off a little at the warehouse but well.. I've already apologised for how that turned out, then that little trip to the library happened and you brought in your folder, I finally had something to go on. Maurice called me in one day and I sat with him and one of his associates named Mary? She was the one who told him all about you, apparently you were researching him in her coffee shop or something?' I couldn't believe it, out of everything that tripped me up, I couldn't help but feel even more bitter about the hipster at Nancy's place that day now, Shane smiled and he continued 'Yeah I couldn't believe it either, didn't seem the type did she? So now he asked me to bring you under control, which as I'm sure you can appreciate, really wasn't good news for either of us, however I continued to play along and I kept feeding Maurice half-truths, that's how he ended up with all your contact details, that day you were all kidnapped and I just so happened to 'show up' that was planned as he needed me to keep you onside too. Everything was planned out by Maurice he was a very intelligent man, however so am I, when I took Aimee to question her, I know how it seemed but I needed to, you see Lance when I had her I slipped a wire into her pocket, she had no idea it was there, so when I let the two of you leave, I informed Maurice where you'd be and when' It started to dawn on me all of a sudden that I was just a pawn in some elaborate game Shane was playing. Shane carried on 'So now I knew Maurice was going to take you both back to the warehouse, he told me to meet him there as he had a job for me, I'd already arranged for some of the other officers to meet me nearby, we were all sat outside listening in to Maurice tell his story, and when all was said and done, I made my entrance I acted the same as I always did and when Maurice gave the order I shot you, I'm sorry, I know it's extreme but I had to, I shot you where I knew it wouldn't kill you if that's any consolation' It wasn't, I was still angry he shot me 'But I'm sure I heard another shot?' I said 'You did, after I shot you, instead of shooting Aimee I shot another round as a signal to the rest of the officers to come in the room, we arrested Maurice there and then and brought you here, Maurice is currently in jail and awaiting trial as we speak'

I was reeling from all the information I had just taken in and I didn't really feel any better knowing any of this, I suppose I was glad that in the end Shane was on the right side otherwise maybe I wouldn't be here to hear any of this right now, however I did have one question left 'Shane, none of this explains why Maurice faked his own death?' Shane stood up and poured himself a glass of water, he took a drink and turned away from me 'Yes, that was a bit of a puzzle to me too, however upon arresting him I had the time to look through his personal belongings, in one of the drawers there were tickets to Italy and Maurice's passport, it looks like Maurice was starting to wrap everything up, I suppose he wanted to live out the rest of his days quietly, that or join the Mafia' Shane laughed at himself. Shane finished his water and headed for the door 'Lance, Maurice would never have been caught if it wasn't for you, thank you' and with that he left, I was pretty sure that was the most sincere Shane had ever been with me. I spent the next week in hospital recovering, I'd requested no more visitors after Shane, I wanted to spend the time reflecting on where I was going or what future I saw for myself.

After leaving the hospital I finally headed home, on my way out the nurse handed me a leather briefcase and told me Shane had left it for me, I didn't open it until I arrived back at my apartment, I sat on the sofa, happy to be back, I place it on the table and opened it up, it was everything I had on Maurice with a note that said 'Hope you don't mind, I've made copies of everything, look forward to reading your article - S.' I'd completely forgotten about my piece this whole time, in fact I'd completely blown work off entirely, I couldn't help but wondered if I even still had a job. I spent a couple of days recovering at home and several hours at my laptop writing about everything that had happened, carefully omitting anything that might have gotten Aimee in any trouble, admittedly it was much harder to type when I could only really use one hand, the nurse had told me I was to keep my left arm in a sling for at least a month, not ideal.

It was a crisp Friday lunch time when I'd finally finished everything, I spent a good 30 minutes showering that morning, hesitant to step back out into the cold, I spent another 15 minutes finding my warmest clothes to ready myself for the bitter cold of the outdoors, I pulled on my coat and grabbed the briefcase which was now holding my finished article. I'd decided to walk to work today, I walked past the spot where we were put in the car by Maurice, made my way down by the river where I met him for the very first time, I could never imagined it turning out the way it did, I walked past Nancy's coffee shop and called in for the usual, it was quiet and Nancy was the only one around 'Nancy, would you mind if we could all meet here tonight at around 7?' I asked, Nancy as kind as always, agreed, I thanked her and left. I got to work and headed straight for the elevator and pressed '45' I was heading straight for Quentin's office, as I approached his door Aimee was at her desk 'Lance, good to see you again' she smiled, I smiled back and asked her if Quentin was free for a moment, she called through and he told her to send me in, I asked her to meet tonight at Nancy's place at 7, she agreed, I headed for Quentin's office. I knocked on the door and he called me in, he gestured to the seat at his desk, he noticed my arm and told me he'd heard but was glad I was ok, he sat down at his desk 'So Lance, why are you here then?' I pulled an envelope out of my bag and handed it to him 'My piece is finished' he took it from me opened up the envelope and pulled it out, we sat there in silence for 20 minutes whilst he read it, I could see he couldn't believe what he was reading from his facial expressions, hopefully the wait was worth it. He finally put it down 'This is incredible, I had no idea this was going on and here I was ready to fire you' I was taken aback by the comment 'You have a great future ahead of you here Lance, I want you to know that' I finally got the recognition I'd craved for so long, but it felt empty, meaningless 'Quentin, this can't be printed until after the outcome of the trial ok?' he nodded in agreement, I reached into my bag once again and handed him another envelope, he took it and opened it 'Is this what you really want?' he asked, I told him it was, he stood up and offered his hand 'I'm sad to see someone with your clear talent leave us like this Lance, but if this is what you want then I accept your resignation' we shook hands and I left, I felt liberated, I said goodbye to Aimee on the way out and headed back for the elevator, I pulled out my phone and sent a message to Shane 'Meet at Nancy's tonight, 7pm'

I arrived at Nancy's place at 6:50pm, everyone else was already there, I wasn't used to being the one people were waiting on, they were all sat around a table and I took a seat with them 'I really appreciate you all meeting up tonight' I started but Aimee cut in 'What's all this about Lance? Quentin told me you quit today? And now this?' she didn't look too happy and upon hearing this Nancy shot me a glance too 'Well, After everything that's happened, I guess this life isn't for me anymore, I don't want to be a journalist anymore and I don't know if I can stay here after all that's happened, so I'm going away for a while and I'm not sure when or if I'll be back, I'm leaving the day after tomorrow I'm going to head back to my parents for a while and then go from there, but I was hoping we could all have 1 last night together as friends before I leave?' They agreed, I don't think they were too happy with me springing this on them like that but I needed to do this for me, no one else. We spent the rest of the evening in the fancy place Aimee took me to, we drank until the early hours and then we all went to get a cab, I embraced them all one last time, and told them to keep in touch, Nancy and Aimee cried, I couldn't help but feel a little emotional too, in all the time I'd been in the city this was the one time I felt like I wasn't alone.

Sunday came and Shane was kind enough to take me to the airport, there was small talk on the way and he promised to keep me in the loop about Maurice's trial, he helped me with my bags out of the car and shook my hand 'Well Lance, I guess this is goodbye, if you ever do decide to come back to Manhattan come see me, I'm confident I could use a man like you on my force' I smiled and thanked him for the offer I headed into the airport and took one last look at the place, at least for now.

It's been 2 months since I left Manhattan I came to my parents and spent some quality time with them, after all I'd never visited since I left the first time around, I caught them up on everything that happened and my arm is back to normal, I kept up with Maurice's trial and it didn't go too well for him, from a man who had it all and was about to head off and live the rest of his days in luxury to a man spending the rest of his life in a federal prison for embezzlement, racketeering, money and drug laundering and various other criminal charges. Shane kept me up to date throughout and told me at the end all the information I had gathered and of course the confession unknowingly recorded by Aimee had been pivotal. Aimee and Nancy have also kept in touch, Nancy is intending on selling up her place and pursuing her artistic dreams and Aimee is still happy where she is as Quentin's PA, I'm happy things have turned out well for both of them. As for me? Well I'm going to spend another month with my parents and then I'm heading out to spend some time with my brother Dan, Coincidentally in Italy, maybe I'll join the mafia I laughed to myself, my thoughts we're interrupted by my phone ringing

'Incoming Call: Unknown'
Strange? I answered 'Hello?'
'Lance Malone, Maurice hasn't forgotten about you, I'll be seeing you'
The line went dead, my body filled with dread, I thought this was over..
I was wrong.

The End

Acknowledgement

To my best friend Johnny, without you I wouldn't have wrote a thing, this short story began just to cheer you up after a challenging few days at work.

Thank you for encouraging me to write.

This ones for you CB.

X

Printed in Great Britain
by Amazon

27326476R00071